M000202025

"A compelling story of love and loss that interweaves the idea of 'what might have been' with 'what is' and leaves readers guessing exactly how one woman's fate will play out until the very last page. A lovely reading escape."

—Casie Bazay, author of *Not Our Summer*

What an oddly wonderful coincidence to discover that our movie, *Peggy Sue Got Married,* inspired writer Shana Schwarz to create her own charming and delightful new book. It's as if *Peggy Sue Got Married* had a child with a new, modern and delightful take on the world. It's time travel revealing the past but excited about the future. Thank you, Shana, for keeping "Stars" twinkling above us.

—Arlene Sarner & Jerry Leichtling, authors of *Peggy Sue Got Married*

AS LONG AS STARS ARE ABOVE YOU

SHANA SCHWARZ

A NineStar Press Publication

www.ninestarpress.com

As Long As Stars Are Above You

First Edition, December 2022

ISBN: 978-1-64890-594-0

Also available in eBook, ISBN: 978-1-64890-593-3

CONTENT WARNING:
This book contains sexual content, which may only be suitable for mature readers. Depictions of illness, medical procedures, and death of a prominent character.

To Mark, Anna, Lucy, and Paul. How long will I love you? Check the cover.

And to Glennon Doyle. Thank you for helping me find my courage to do the hard things.

even an afterthought in his mind, but an incomplete one.

Maybe we can talk when I get back?" she suggested, still trying
ch his eye.

A reaction from Dan, finally, as he looked up at her for a mo-
t with a haunted expression.

"Whatever you think. We probably should..."

What he thought they probably should discuss, however, he
dn't say. He and his phone headed toward the guest bathroom
fore she'd even had a chance to kiss him goodbye.

Joey hated herself for thinking it, but she missed how they used
o fight. She could deal with anger. But this? This was apathy. Anger, at least, meant he still cared.

His words bounced around inside her head as she finished
getting ready, and they were still on repeat as she wound her car
through the familiar streets of their old neighborhood. As she
turned the engine off and gave herself a once-over in the rearview
mirror, she hoped the few tears she couldn't blink back hadn't
messed up her mascara too much.

Not that it mattered. When Joey Shaw walked into a room,
people always seemed to notice. It wasn't that she was pretty. She
was, but she carried herself like she wasn't, so sometimes people
forgot she was almost striking.

It was more that people could sense she'd entered a room, so
they always turned to look. She brought with her a sense of...de-
light? Was that the right word? A sense that the room would be

CHAPTER ONE

"WHATEVER."

There it was again. That word. Dan tried to make it seem
a positive thing, as if letting her decide everything was a courte
But all she heard was him pulling away, literally. Shutting down.

"Well, I guess I could go on my own?" Joey said, hoping he'
hear how much she didn't want that to be the case.

Fight for me, she pleaded silently to the back of Dan's head.
Remind me that I'm not in this alone.

"I don't care, Jo, really. We need to talk, but just tell me if I
need to get dressed or..."

He didn't finish the sentence but drifted back to looking at his
phone. Apparently, that's how little she meant to him now. She

different now she was in it. She wasn't loud and she'd never purposely sought attention, but she made people feel good, and that was a welcome addition to any room.

*

THIS FEELING WAS usually magnified by the fact Joey typically entered rooms with Dan. Everyone also noticed when Dan entered a room, and there was no confusion about it being a feeling. Dan was beautiful and impossible to ignore. He was kind and had the same air of what we'll call delightfulness as Joey had, but it was his looks people noticed first.

Thus, when Joey walked into her twenty-year high school reunion, everyone did their typical noticing, then also craned their necks for a glimpse of Dan.

But Dan was not there.

Word quickly spread through the gymnasium that Joey Shaw had entered Dan-less and even though Joey knew it would happen, she prickled with indignation and felt herself losing the will to be her typical self. Dan hadn't even gone to Conquistador High School. That hadn't stopped everyone at her school from knowing who he was while she attended, and the fact they'd been together since basically kindergarten had just led everyone to assume they'd show up to the reunion together.

Maybe that was why, on top of everything else they were dealing with, Joey had given Dan the option to skip the reunion, at least the evening festivities. Sure, they'd show up tomorrow with the kids to the family picnic, but Joey was tired of dragging this new, sad Dan places he clearly didn't want to be.

The gym was decorated to look exactly as it had for one of their dances back in 2002 and Joey smiled as her eyes adjusted to the dim lighting and the full picture came into view. Duke Photography had set up a cheesy backdrop for pictures, twinkle lights crisscrossed over the dance floor, round tables with plastic covers made a semicircle around the room, and approximately five people were on the dance floor while the band played "Love Shack" from a slightly raised platform directly across from her.

Joey relaxed a little as she took in her sister, Betty, on that stage, wearing her best early aughts attire, then groaned as she realized the clothes were actually from those years and still fit her younger, beautiful sister. Betty and her roommate, Rachel, made up half of an all-girl cover band called the Lovely Ritas, and they were all gorgeous, talented, and single. Joey could already see some of her male classmates trying to sneak looks at them while their wives sent daggers Betty's way. She hoped they were coming up on a break soon so she could tell Betty that Johnny Sanglin, whom they'd both had crushes on in high school, was openly staring at her, much to the chagrin of his wife.

Even though it had been her idea to show up alone, Joey immediately questioned that decision as a group of women waved at her and she realized she couldn't think of any of their names. Dan was always so good at remembering names. Even at a school he didn't attend, Joey bet he'd have had at least half of their names locked and loaded or would have been able to charmingly ask for them in order to cover for her.

In an effort to pretend she hadn't seen them, Joey took a sharp right and headed for the snack and drinks table, set up where it always had been at school events, but then noticed the tent next to it that she'd never seen before.

MADAME FATE, FORTUNE TELLER: SEE YOUR FUTURE read a banner pinned above the entrance.

Joey knew exactly what her future held, and it wasn't good. Everything with Dan had been accelerating at a pace she knew she couldn't control and the last thing she needed was a reminder of that. But the group of women whose names she couldn't remember had moved in her direction, and as her normal charm and wit felt out of reach at that moment, she grabbed one of the available glasses of wine from the table and quickly stepped into the tent.

"*Haalllo*, you have come to see vat your future holds?"

Joey tried not to laugh. She failed. A woman dressed like Professor Trelawney sitting at a tiny card table hit her with a booming voice and terrible Russian accent as the tent flaps closed behind her. The tent was bigger than it looked from the outside and was cut off in the middle by a divider just behind Madam Fate.

"Uh, no, actually," said Joey. "I was just looking for a place to drink this and hide for a minute, if that's okay?"

Madam Fate furrowed her eyebrows and looked Joey up and down.

"Sit." She pointed to the chair opposite her, the accent suddenly gone. "You're the first one in here all night. I'm Mary. Mary Fate."

Joey laughed again, but this time with Mary, as the latter reached into a bag and pulled out a flask. Joey sat across from her and they both said cheers before taking large gulps of their respective drinks.

"I actually am good at this stuff," Mary said. "But some people like the whole character thing, so I go with it. You sure you don't want me to tell you anything about what's coming?"

"I came here tonight to forget about what's coming." Joey finished her glass of wine with another swig. "I thought it might be fun to remember back when life was easier, you know? Back when I stupidly believed...back when things weren't so..."

Mary gave her a few seconds to finish the thought, then said, "Can I see your hand?"

The wine was making everything a little fuzzy, and since Mary had dropped the whole crazy act, Joey obliged, and placed her hand into the fortune teller's palm.

"Ahh, I see what the problem is." Mary was still looking intently into Joey's hand.

"I need to moisturize more often?"

"That wouldn't hurt," Mary said with a laugh. It was a light, airy laugh that suddenly jarred something in Joey. She couldn't remember the last time she had laughed like that.

"You married the wrong person," Mary told her. "I mean, it's fine, but there is someone else who you're supposed to be with and that's why everything feels wrong."

The words sucked the air out of the small tent and Joey tried to pull her hand back, but Mary held it tighter. Who the hell did this woman think she was? She and Dan had three beautiful kids and a life most people would envy, and sure, things lately were, well, not good, but...

"The valentine," Mary said. "Who gave you the valentine?"

"What did you say?" Joey gasped.

"You were supposed to end up with the one who gave you the valentine." Mary traced a spot on Joey's hand with her fingernail. "Do you want to see what could have been?"

"What are you talking about? Who told you about that valentine?" Joey stood and this time pulled her hand sharply back from Mary's grip, nearly stumbling backward in the process. The tent was warm, and the wine had hit her quickly on an empty stomach.

"It's okay, Joey," Mary said, now looking at her with concern. "Behind this screen, you can see your past. Do you want a chance to make some changes?"

It's just a screen. This woman is crazy. I've never told anyone about that valentine. What in the hell is going on?

Joey's thoughts were swirling, and she knew she had to get out of the tent, but she could hear voices near the entrance and didn't want to burst out on the verge of tears. Every teenage insecurity came rushing back and her number one rule had always been to not stand out. There was only one option to exit, so she told herself it was just a screen, this was all pretend, and ignored Mary's outstretched hand to steady herself before taking a step forward—

Then everything went dark.

CHAPTER TWO

WHEN JOEY OPENED her eyes again, she knew she must be in the hospital and had likely been heavily sedated. What else could explain how well rested she felt? And that back pain she woke up with every day? Gone. Damn. They must have given her some good pain meds.

But when she looked around for signs that she had, indeed, been taken somewhere for help, she instead decided she must have died. She'd always wondered what heaven would look like and was immediately disappointed to discover it looked like her childhood bedroom.

I was hoping for Disneyland, she thought, taking in the full view around her.

Yes, this was definitely her childhood bedroom, just as she'd left it. For starters, she was lying on a waterbed. She rolled to her right and felt the familiar slosh of water and saw the assortment of pictures, books, and knickknacks decorating her bed's built-in bookshelf. A picture of her and Betty dressed as princesses from her favorite Halloween, one of her and Dan at prom, and a framed shot of the three of them the day she got her driver's license.

As she turned to see the wall opposite her bed, she realized something felt a little different. She reached down and laughed as her hands discovered two small, perky boobs, quite the difference from the large, post-motherhood ones she'd been carrying around for years. But wait, that must also mean...ah yes, her hands went further down to discover a tiny, flat stomach and an equally small pair of thighs.

How did I ever think I was fat, she sighed, remembering hours spent agonizing that she didn't look exactly like the Calvin Klein underwear models who frequented her *Cosmopolitan* magazines. Well, if heaven was her childhood room, it kinda made sense that she had her old body back.

She stood up and was amazed to feel the floor under her feet. She kinda thought she'd float, but maybe that came later? She felt her arms, and everything appeared to be pretty solid. Maybe this was some sort of processing center, like in *Chances Are?* Yeah, that would make sense. Maybe when you die, they send you somewhere familiar first, so you don't freak out. She was really starting to figure out this whole "being dead" thing.

Figuring it all out made sense, because she also felt mentally clear for the first time in...forever? She felt like she could do calculus again and it would all just click. This also made sense; as she had her high school body back, the brain had come with it. And, oh, what a brain it had been.

It's not that she wasn't a smart adult. Sure, she'd felt pretty dumb when the kids were little and they sucked every spare brain cell from her during the years of sleepless nights, breastfeeding, endless laundry, and *Yo Gabba Gabba!*. But even as they had gotten older, the brain she'd been so famous for as a kid always felt just slightly out of reach.

But now, in this weird limbo state she seemed to have found herself in, she could feel synapses connecting that hadn't done so in decades. Which is why not being able to figure out how she'd gotten here was so jarring.

Thinking about it logically, she could remember every moment of being in the tent. It had felt warmer and warmer, but that was partially the wine. Or had it been the beginning of a heart attack? No, surely, there would have been some pain. There was something about going behind a screen. Then the panic because a stranger had told her she'd married the wrong person.

Dan. Had she left Dan behind? And the kids?

Before the weight of that thought could fully register, a knock on the door pulled her back to reality. Or whatever this new reality was, anyway.

"Just making sure you're up, sleepyhead," came a voice from behind the door.

"Dad?" she choked out, suddenly aware she could speak.

But whomever had spoken to her had moved on. She could hear feet shuffling through the house. A clock on her nightstand said 7:30 a.m. Her alarm had always been set for 7:32, a weird quirk because she loved numbers that were divisible by three, but that hadn't stopped her dad from knocking a few minutes early every day. It had bugged her then, but the memory of it now made her oddly happy. Or the experience. This wasn't a memory; it had just happened. Or had it?

If she could hear things outside this room, it stood to reason there were other things outside this room. This felt both logical and illogical at the same time. She could stand, she could talk. What else could she do?

She sat down at her desk and moved the mouse next to her teal iMac. The screen woke up, so she opened a document.

"I need to make a list," she said out loud, again testing that her vocal cords worked.

She made a column and titled it "Evidence I Am Dead." Underneath, she began to type:

> *Have magically returned to being a teenager*
> *Felt a little funny at reunion*

Family history of heart disease

No one knows what heaven is like; this could be it

Back doesn't hurt

She scrunched her nose and looked at the list. Any good scientist would now test their hypothesis, but another thought nagged at her. What had Mary said? Something about seeing what her life could have been like? She made a second column and titled it "Evidence I Have Time Traveled."

Have magically returned to being a teenager

Back doesn't hurt

Have read extensively about time travel and it takes many forms

Crazy woman in tent alluded to similar scenario

I appear to be fully corporeal

This doesn't feel like heaven

Joey looked at both lists for a few minutes, back and forth, as she tried to make sense of them or come up with a third, more logical answer. If she had gone back in time, what day had she gone back to? She stood up to shake out her hands, and looked around her room a bit more, hoping another clue might catch her eye. She opened her closet, saw a long, black robe hanging first in line, and gasped.

It could only be one day, and it was the most fateful of her life.

CHAPTER THREE

MAY 15, 2002! It had to be! She had picked up her cap and gown the day before graduation and had obviously only worn it that day.

Suddenly, option two felt like the only thing that made sense. Heaven couldn't be some sort of *Groundhog Day* thing that made her relive this day over and over. It had been a good day, but her high school graduation wouldn't have cracked the top five for the best in her life. In fact, it had been kind of ordinary, up until the end.

So ordinary, in fact, that she realized she typically couldn't remember what she had done until the evening. Or, at least, her grown-up self couldn't remember, which she knew because the kids had asked her for details dozens of times over the years.

Think, Joey! she commanded. Now she was in possession of her teenage brain, the memories of that day started to materialize.

It was hot, because it was Phoenix in May, but not terrible. She remembered the weather because her whole family had gone for a walk that morning. Wow—how long had it been since she'd remembered that? It was such an eventful day, but that walk had been the last one they'd taken, just the four of them, and Joey was thrilled at the thought of reliving this day in particular. She made a mental note to put one point in the heaven column.

Dad had suggested a family walk because it was Joey's big day and he thought it would be nice to spend time together. He'd seemed a little emotional, but Dad always got emotional on big occasions, and Joey's mind had been so focused on her speech that she hadn't taken the time to really think about what that walk meant until, well, now. Dad must have known what was coming that night but didn't want to spoil the surprise.

And so, they had gone on a walk, with Betty rambling about her plans for the summer. They were both going back to NAU Summer Music Camp, Betty as a camper and Joey as a counselor. Betty was overly chatty, and Joey wondered if her little sister hadn't also been sad that she was graduating and moving out soon, with excessive chattiness as her way of hiding her emotions.

Then there was Mom. Mom had walked a few steps behind her girls, taking it all in with her usual "how did this all go so fast?" energy. She'd suggested they sing a few songs along the way; Joey and Betty had obliged.

Before the walk, Joey had suggested they stop next door to see if Dan wanted to go, but Mom said he wasn't home. They all could have seen his car wasn't in the driveway, and Joey never questioned how Mom somehow knew that before they'd gone out, but now it all seemed so clear.

Dan was picking up Joey's engagement ring. Her mom and dad both knew, maybe Betty did too.

She began to wonder why none of them told her. Sure, it was obvious where they were heading, but Joey had been a little blind-sided that he'd decided to propose the night she graduated from high school. Didn't anyone think they were too young? But when she looked around and saw both of their families surrounding them, eyes aglow with happy tears, everything seemed so predestined that she'd said yes without really even thinking.

Everything that came after felt the same way. If they were engaged, why not move in together? And since they were both going to ASU, why not get a little place near campus? And why drag out an engagement, when a wedding is such a fun event, and who knows how much longer some of our older relatives might be here?

She'd always looked back on this date as monumental because it was the day she'd gotten engaged, but suddenly it felt like the most cosmically important date in her entire life. No wonder Madam Fate had sent her back here.

Wait, was she really already believing that? *Madam Fate was just a woman named Mary with a silly accent in a silly tent. Fortune telling isn't real, and neither is this kind of magic.*

And yet, here she was. In her old room with her old body on a day where just a few things going differently could change the entire course of her life. She knew exactly how things would play out if she followed the course. She knew happiness awaited her down the path she'd originally chosen. Sure, pain was coming in about twenty years, but she and Dan had built something amazing. She remembered how much Mary's words about marrying the wrong person had hurt.

But what was it Mary had said about that valentine? As much as her logical brain wanted to dismiss everything else, Joey couldn't shake the feeling that everything she was experiencing hinged on that one point.

On Valentine's Day twenty-one years ago...or, she guessed, last year, if she was really back in 2002, she'd received her usual assortment of valentines. Student council organized a Valentine-gram program every year where students could send each other a little card and gift as part of a fundraiser. As junior class treasurer, she helped organize it every year, then helped deliver the grams during third period. Dan usually asked Betty or someone to buy one for her, and she always exchanged them with a few other friends too.

When she got back to English class after delivering the ones assigned to her, she found her desk covered with red and pink construction paper cards, heart-shaped suckers, and a teddy bear holding a jewelry box. Dan had sent her music note earrings with the bear, and the candy ones had come from the usual suspects, but one was left unsigned.

> *Dear Joey, I've had a crush on you for years and have been too shy to tell you in person. I think you're amazing. I'll be under the big tree behind the gym after school if you want to say hi.*

Joey had blushed, then immediately shoved the valentine in her backpack. Everyone knew she had a boyfriend. Even if Dan didn't go to Conquistador, he was around at school functions enough to make it clear to the rest of the boys in her school that she was off-limits. She preferred it that way. While other girls in her class primped and stressed over how they looked at school, being Dan's girlfriend had afforded her a certain status that helped her feel like she could just focus on her studies. She'd had her sights set on valedictorian, and who needed all that drama?

As the day went on, though, she couldn't help but wonder who would be so bold as to send her such a note. That was pretty mature writing for most boys her age.

The thought made her grab the card back out of her bag. She smoothed it out and studied it, hoping no one in her chemistry class would notice. The handwriting was loopy and romantic, with little hearts over each letter *I*. Not only was it too mature for boys her age to have written, the penmanship was like none she'd ever seen from the guys at her school.

Her logical brain made the only conclusion it could: her secret admirer was a girl.

Chapter Four

IF MARY WAS right, not only should she have not married Dan, she shouldn't have married a man at all.

But Mary wasn't right, she nearly shouted inside her head.

And besides, she didn't even know who had sent the valentine.

Okay, she'd always had her suspicions, but that's all they'd ever been. Short of comparing writing samples from all the girls in the school, she'd basically had no way to figure out who had sent it. Instead of stopping by the tree behind the gym after school that day, Joey had chickened out and walked to the front of the school instead. She did look around and try to see who might be missing, but in the chaos of teenage drivers peeling out of the parking lot while everyone shuffled off to afterschool activities, it was impossible to tell.

I have a boyfriend, I have a boyfriend, she told herself as she resisted the urge to run in the opposite direction. And it was true. She and Dan and Betty had been inseparable since her family had moved in next door to his house the summer before she started kindergarten. Going back to see who had a crush on her felt akin to cheating, by high school terms anyway. And the fact she was pretty sure it was a girl felt...exhilarating.

No, not that. It felt...wrong, right? She was in love with Dan and that meant she was straight. It didn't matter that she had always thought girls were beautiful. They were the fairer sex, after all. And didn't everyone have a crush on Jennifer Aniston?

Wait, not a crush. Joey just really loved her on *Friends* and wanted to be like her. Not, like, be with her.

Sitting in her childhood room, Joey felt a rush of those old feelings come back. She had told Dan over the years about women she'd found attractive, and he was always intrigued, but she'd laughed it off as something she could only share with him because he was her husband and best friend. Taking the thoughts any further than that would be admitting what she'd tried really hard to ignore since middle school.

When she and Dan were fourteen, their friendship had blossomed into the proverbial something more. Suddenly, having him over for sleepovers, like they had when they were kids, was tense. Betty had always had a crush on Dan, but she was boy crazy years before her tomboy sister. It wasn't until they watched *Casper* together one night and Joey looked down to see Dan's hand holding hers that she realized the butterflies she felt when he was around were something more than the junk food and soda swirling around her stomach.

Betty cried for days when Joey told her she and Dan had kissed at the park one day, but she wrote some of her best songs that summer and won a prize at camp. And besides, everyone could see that Joey and Dan belonged together, so what did the hurt feelings of a little sister mean when compared to destiny?

But that same year, Joey had roomed at camp with Taylor Page, arguably the coolest girl in their school. Taylor was kind to Joey and even let her tag along to the social events during camp, but Joey was infatuated and terribly confused whenever they hung out. Where Joey was well-liked, Taylor was adored. Surely, Joey was responding to that same energy, she told herself. Taylor was the same age as Joey, but her body looked...not like Joey's. Pictures of them together looked like Barbie and Skipper.

Taylor wasn't popular like the other girls in school. She was an incredibly talented cellist, and everyone knew she was going to be a professional musician someday. She was shy, but easy to talk to once you could get her going. Talent, beauty, and humility are basically the trifecta to make up the coolest girl at camp.

On the last night of camp, Joey and Taylor stayed up late, chatting about how camp had gone, and what school would be like that year. They'd gone to school together for years, but as high school loomed, they knew things would be different, especially as some of their classmates went to other schools, and kids from other schools joined them at Conquistador.

"Are you worried you'll miss Dan?" Taylor asked, as they sat together in Joey's bed, sharing a bag of popcorn.

"Nah," said Joey. "I see him every day. I mean, I like having him around at school, but it's okay."

"Yeah. I get it. I'm going to miss Melanie though."

Melanie was Taylor's best friend. Her family and Dan's had both opted to send them to a smaller, private school that specialized in science. Joey was good at science but had no desire to focus on it when she was just as good at other subjects. Taylor struggled in most classes, but since she'd probably get a scholarship for music, she'd decided to stick with the public school option too.

"Do you want to play Truth or Dare?" Taylor asked.

"Just the two of us?" Joey said. "Or do you want to go see who else is up?"

"Nah, just us," Taylor laughed. "Maybe I'll dare you to go wake someone up at some point."

They both laughed and turned to face each other on the bed.

"You first," said Joey. "Truth or dare?"

"Truth."

"What size bra do you wear?" Joey asked, realizing she felt bold after three Cherry Cokes.

"Ha," said Taylor. "Um, I guess a C? I was a B, but they're kinda tight, so, yeah, C."

"You're so lucky. I wear an A, but there's not much there."

"You'll get them and you'll hate them. They get in the way of my cello."

A fit of giggles hit them both before Taylor said, "Okay, truth or dare?"

"Truth."

"Do you like girls, or just boys?" Taylor asked, her face suddenly serious.

"Oh, uh, boys. You mean like like, right?"

"Yeah. I didn't know if you just like Dan, or maybe if you've ever had a crush on a girl...like I have."

It was the first time a friend had ever shared something so intimate with her and Joey knew in that moment a good friend should make Taylor feel okay about the whole thing. She knew this, but it didn't stop her from blurting out, " *You're gay?*"

Taylor looked taken aback, giving Joey a second to bring her original, kinder reaction to the surface.

"I mean, cool. That's cool. You like girls. Okay."

"Yeah," said Taylor. "Johnny Sanglin kissed me after the dance this year and it just kinda hit me. Plus, I think I'm in love with Jennifer Aniston."

"Me too!" Joey exclaimed.

"Johnny kissed you?" Taylor asked.

"Oh, er, no. I meant I love Jennifer Aniston."

"But you said you only like boys."

"Well, I thought you only liked boys. I thought you and Johnny were kind of a thing?"

"No, we're not, but you could have told me you like girls like that, even if you didn't think I did. I mean, I just told you."

"I'm sorry." Joey was confused. "I guess I don't really know. I know how I feel about Dan, but maybe..."

"Maybe?" Taylor said.

"Uh, I think it's your turn. Truth or dare?"

"Dare."

And maybe it was the caffeine buzz, or maybe it was the darkness in the dorm room they shared, lit only by the nightlight Joey had packed. Or maybe it was Taylor's C-cup breasts that Joey had been darting glances at as they sat perfectly underneath her pajama top for the past two weeks. But whatever it was, something told Joey it was now or never. So, she went with now.

"I dare you, to, uh..."

As she leaned forward to kiss Taylor, Joey was thrilled to see Taylor leaning in too. Their lips met, then they pulled apart, both shyly glancing away.

"I've never done that before," Joey admitted.

"Me either," said Taylor.

"You said you like girls."

"Well, yeah, but I hadn't kissed anyone yet. Here." Taylor

stood and pulled Joey to her feet.

They bumped noses as Taylor kissed Joey again, but this time they both opened their mouths and *really* kissed, doing their best to emulate what they'd seen in TV shows and movies. The boldness Joey had felt earlier came back and she raised one hand and placed it softly on Taylor's breast, before panicking and putting it back down by her side.

They both pulled away from each other, but this time were brave enough to hold their gaze, a little breathless from the kissing.

"Yeah, I'm definitely gay," said Taylor with a smile. "That was so much better than kissing Johnny."

"I'm...I'm..." Joey struggled for words. Was that better than kissing Dan? The word *no* came to her before she could even finish the question. Kissing Taylor felt amazing, but so did kissing Dan. Dan! She had just cheated on her very first boyfriend. And she'd done it by kissing a girl and touching her boob.

"Joey, it's okay," Taylor said. "Just think of that as helping a friend figure something out. Really. I won't ever tell anyone."

Joey's mind was racing. Is that what she wanted? She was in love with Dan in the way only a fourteen-year-old girl can be in love and didn't want to ruin that, but all she wanted to do in that moment was to keep kissing Taylor and maybe, just maybe...touch her other boob? Ugh, she was a monster.

"It'll be our secret, I promise," Taylor said, stepping forward to brush Joey's hair out of her face. "I really like you, Joey, but I've had months to think this through. I'm not ready to come out to the other kids at camp or school and you don't have to decide anything right now. It's so much more than just having a crush on someone. You know what other people are going to say when they find out."

Joey knew in an instant it wasn't just Taylor's body that was more mature. She really knew herself, and, sadly, knew what she'd be facing if she were to tell people she was gay. Joey didn't even know another gay person, come to think of it. And as her one goal in life was to not stand out, suddenly being half of the only lesbian couple at Conquistador High School felt like the wrong path.

And so, they hugged and climbed into their beds that night, never to speak of what had happened again.

Until, perhaps, a certain valentine?

CHAPTER FIVE

JOEY HAD ALWAYS suspected Taylor had sent the valentine, and now it seemed clearer than ever. She'd looked for Taylor after school that day and was pretty sure she hadn't seen her. Was it because Taylor had been waiting for her behind the gym? Had she left her friend there, sad and alone, on Valentine's Day?

Taylor had made it all the way through high school without anyone finding out her secret. Joey never told a soul, and she pretended to be surprised when she heard years later that Taylor had come out after landing a spot in some fancy Paris orchestra after attending a conservatory in Europe. She'd never even told Dan. He wouldn't have been judgmental or anything, but she couldn't figure out a way to tell him what she knew without sharing how she knew it.

Joey and Dan had been famous for being each other's first and only everything. People thought it was so neat that they were each other's first kisses and they were the perfect high school sweetheart couple, eventually getting married and only being with each other. "You mean you've never kissed another man?" new friends would ask Joey in shock and amusement.

And since Taylor had been the only other person she'd kissed, she'd answered honestly while keeping her secret safe for decades.

Joey opened her closet again and found a box of keepsakes stuffed in underneath old yearbooks and other scholastic detritus. Inside the box, she found school music performance programs, notes passed between her and friends between classes, and a pile of Valentine-grams from over the years. On the very bottom, still wrinkled from its original crumpling, lay the one she'd gotten last year. She opened it and pictured Taylor writing it. She had been so brave to put her feelings down on paper and to try to let Taylor know she still felt those feelings, even after all these years.

Okay, only four years, but that's a lot when you're eighteen.

Joey began to search her brain again. What would Taylor have been doing today? She only lived a few streets away, and Joey pictured herself showing up on her doorstep, holding the valentine and saying...what?

"Hey, it's me, Joey! I actually am bi, and I'd love to kiss you and touch your other boob?"

No, that wasn't right. It was definitely what she wanted to say, but she couldn't reference the valentine without explaining why she suddenly knew how significant it was. And saying they should get married after only speaking as friends/acquaintances all through high school felt absurd.

If she was remembering correctly, Taylor would be leaving that night for Europe. Everyone had talked about how glamorous it was that she'd be skipping the graduation party to start her conservatory program early. At the senior yearbook signing party, Joey had asked Taylor a bit about it and remembered two things: she was going to live in London for school and she was really nervous to be going alone.

Was that what she was sent back here for? To go with Taylor and save her from that loneliness? They'd lost touch through the years, but Joey had heard things were going well for Taylor. She was pretty sure she'd even gotten married to a woman and had no reason to think things were anything but perfect for her.

But wouldn't people say the same thing about her and Dan? And as only she knew, things were far from perfect for her in 2022.

Joey sat back down and looked at her list. This was definitely not heaven, so she erased that column. If she had time traveled here, certainly she could time travel back. But how?

Mary Fate. If Mary had sent her here, surely she could send her back, right? She opened up her internet browser and waited while it loaded. Then she remembered she was in 2002 and this was going to take a minute, so she walked to her closet to get dressed for the walk she now knew was coming. As she sat back down, she wondered if Google was a thing yet, and typed it into the address bar. It opened but looked nothing how she knew it would in 2022.

I should invest in Google, she thought to herself as she typed "Mary Fate" into the search field. A crude but working webpage was the only result and Joey laughed as she saw a young Mary's picture slowly load on the screen. Apparently, she'd invented the Madam Fate persona somewhere between now and the now Joey had just come from, but she did have an address in Phoenix where it said she offered various psychic services, including parties. Joey jotted it down and set it on her dresser.

She then searched for flights leaving Phoenix that night for London, called the only company that had one (British Airways), used the credit card she'd opened last year for emergencies, and booked herself a one-way ticket.

She wasn't quite sure yet that she'd use it, but it was better to have it, just in case. And if she had a plane ticket, she should probably also pack. She looked around at her room and wanted to cry. When she lived this date the first time, she'd been so focused on her graduation that night she'd forgotten to say goodbye to her room, her childhood. She had assumed she'd have the whole summer before moving out into a dorm and would spend late nights with Betty, eating junk food and watching old movies.

But in addition to a ring, Dan was probably also putting the deposit down on the apartment they were going to rent. It was such a Dan move. He realized if they signed a one-year lease when school started in August, they'd have to renew that month every year. If they moved out in May, the lease would be up when they graduated in exactly four years, because of course they'd graduate on time.

And they had graduated on time, so it worked out perfectly, but that was beside the point. Joey had been so excited to be out on her own and living with Dan that she'd missed out on giving her family a proper goodbye. Sure, they'd still seen each other often, but it wasn't the same after she moved out. For someone who loved Peter Pan as much as Joey did, she'd grown up too quickly. And sure, she had loved being a young mother and that felt like getting a second childhood, but when you go to bed stressed about bills and exhausted from chasing toddlers all day, no amount of playtime during the day can keep you from feeling old.

Joey quickly threw her favorite clothes and shoes into a suitcase and decided she'd buy whatever else she needed once she got to London, if that's what she actually ended up doing. She found her passport and searched the pile of papers on her desk for her acceptance letter to the London School of Creative Writing. She hadn't even told Dan she'd applied, let alone been accepted, and managed to secure a student visa without her parents knowing either. Smart, logical Joey knew her full ride at Arizona State University was the most sensible option. She and Dan had both gotten degrees without incurring any student debt and moving to London would cost a fortune, but she still couldn't help applying and dreaming of living abroad.

Maybe she hadn't time traveled just to see what her life would be like with Taylor. Maybe she was meant to live an entirely different life, after all, and maybe stepping into that tent wasn't some random occurrence.

Maybe it was Fate.

CHAPTER SIX

PACKED AND BRIMMING with excitement, Joey finally stepped out into the hallway of her parents' house. To her right, she could hear the radio in her mom's bathroom playing the KEZ morning show with Beth and Bill, familiar voices she'd heard most mornings for as long as she could remember. Instead, she turned left and found Betty in their shared bathroom, brushing her teeth and looking adorable in mismatched pajamas and braces.

"Hey, kiddo," Joey said, realizing a little too late she never would have called her sister that.

"Hey, it's the graduate!" Betty spat one last gob of toothpaste into the sink. "Doo do doo do doo do doo...and here's to you, Mrs. Robinson!" she sang, in her best Simon and Garfunkel impression.

"You know that's about an older woman who seduces her daughter's boyfriend, right?" Joey laughed and opened her arms to Betty for a hug.

"You know I don't care, right?" Her sister bounced toward Joey to accept the offer.

"I do." Joey petted her sister's curls.

"Hey, you okay?" Betty asked, still resting her head on Joey's shoulder. "I mean, it is a big day."

Joey took a step back and stared at her sister.

She knows, Joey realized. If she wasn't sure before, she definitely was now. Everyone in her family knew what was coming tonight and she'd missed all the signs. For someone as smart as she was, she'd been pretty oblivious.

"I'm more than okay," she said, pulling Betty in for a hug. "I've got the best little sister in the world."

Betty tried to laugh this off and pull away, but Joey wouldn't let her.

If this is our last day together before everything changes, I'm going to cherish it.

"Aww! My girls," Joey's mom said, coming into the hallway. "Am I interrupting a moment?"

"Do I hear my girls all gathered?"

Joey laughed as her dad's voice boomed from his office and he stepped into the space, filling the doorframe. Then she tried not to cry realizing how young he and her mom looked.

"Hey, how about we go for a walk?" she said, her voice cracking just a bit.

"That's what I was going to suggest!" Her dad clapped her on the back. "Gotta get those pre-graduation jitters out, don't we?"

"Nah, I'm not nervous," Joey lied. "I've got my speech all prepared."

"Even better!" her dad said.

The four of them scattered to get shoes on and Joey took a minute to look out of the side window in the family room. Sure enough, Dan's car wasn't in the driveway. She had hoped suggesting the walk herself would get them all out early enough to catch him, but it looked like he'd already left for the day to put his proposal plan into motion.

As sure as she was that she was supposed to be following an alternate plan, the thought of Dan's disappointment tonight left her full of dread. He was her best friend in the world, and she loved him more than anything, save the three kids they'd created. Even knowing where things were headed, could she really knowingly change both of their lives like this?

"Spying on your booooyfriend?"

Her mom's singsong voice floated into the room as she dropped her hands from the blinds.

"Do you know where he is?" Joey asked.

"Oh, er, is he not home?"

"He's not," said Joey, impressed with her mother's

commitment to not give up Dan's secret.

"Maybe he's out getting ready for his own graduation?" Her mom was good. In addition to taking care of everything for Joey's graduation that day, Dan was probably also out picking up his own cap and gown. His graduation was the following day, thus her mom managed to avoid telling what she knew and also not lie.

Before Joey could come up with another way to get information from her family, Betty and her dad walked in, all ready to go for their walk. And thus, out they went.

They took the same route Joey remembered them taking before, but this time, she tried to really notice all the little things. The way her dad smiled at the three of them, clearly beaming with pride. Or the way she and Betty could harmonize just right on each song their mom called out for them to sing. It was effortless. It was the same energy she'd carried into her own family with Dan and as much as she was trying not to think of her kids, she couldn't help but picture their faces as she walked.

She knew in that moment she couldn't run away with Taylor that night, and just happened to have the realization right in front of Taylor's house. She wondered if she was maybe just supposed to talk to Taylor, to acknowledge the valentine for once and for all. Maybe that was the closure they both needed, then she could go find Mary Fate and go back to her real life.

"Hey, guys, I'm going to stop and say hi to Taylor for a sec. I'll catch up," Joey said, stopping in her tracks.

"Okie dokie," her dad said. "We'll head to the end of the street to grab the mail and circle back this way for you."

As the rest of her family went off without her, Joey walked quickly up to Taylor's house. She was on a mission and knocked three times before she could change her mind.

Taylor answered the door, still in her pajamas, and Joey flashed back to that night in camp. Joey had finally caught up to Taylor, height-wise, but Taylor was even curvier and more beautiful than she'd been before. She'd tried not to look at her for four years as they got through high school, but she couldn't help gaping at her now.

"Hey, Joey!" Taylor said. "Excited for tonight?"

"Oh, er, yeah," Joey said. "You?"

"Nervous. But yeah. Excited, I guess."

"Can I talk to you for a sec?"

"Oh sure." Taylor stepped aside. "Come on in."

Joey walked into Taylor's house and immediately regretted it. The news that she wasn't going to run away with her would sound insane. Asking about the valentine seemed borderline cruel, all of a sudden. Why had she come up here?

"I think I know what this is about," said Taylor. "I was hoping Dan would talk to you."

"Dan?"

"Yeah, about the mix-up? He said he'd let you know." Taylor was searching Joey's face for some kind of understanding, but it most certainly wasn't there, so she continued. "The London School of Creative Writing is connected to my conservatory. They sent a letter to Conquistador to let us know we'd both been offered full scholarships, but yours went to his address. He brought it to me because he thought there was a mix-up, but I said I already had mine, so you must have applied too."

Every ounce of oxygen in Joey's body seemed to leave her at that moment. Dan knew about London? She'd been offered a scholarship and he hadn't told her?

It didn't make sense to her until suddenly it did. He hadn't proposed because he was eager to marry her. He proposed so that she wouldn't leave.

CHAPTER SEVEN

"ARE YOU OKAY?" Taylor asked. She'd asked it a few times, but Joey hadn't heard her until around ask number three.

"I can't believe this," Joey said. "I can't believe he would do that."

"He didn't tell you?" Taylor sounded disbelieving. "I was sure he would give you the letter. I told him to tell you we could make plans together, but when I didn't hear from you, I just assumed..."

"No, he, uh, didn't tell me." Tears filled Joey's eyes.

Her entire marriage had been built on a lie. Dan didn't trust her to make her own decision and didn't trust that their relationship could survive long distance. He didn't even give her the chance to have a conversation about it. What if she didn't even want to go to

London?

"Oh Joey, I'm so sorry," Taylor said. "I should have asked, but you knew I was going to school there and never mentioned you'd applied, so I figured you decided to just stay here."

Her words floated like a dialogue bubble above Joey's head as she tried to make sense of everything. She knew she'd gotten in and hadn't really made plans to go to London. Hadn't she already chosen Dan by default? No, not default. She loved him. They were best friends and her first and only love.

But would a best friend keep a secret like that?

To be fair, she'd also kept a secret from him for years. Also involving Taylor. Sheesh, what was it with this girl?

Joey looked at Taylor and tried to picture them together in London. There were so many question marks, but maybe that was better than a life completely decided for her. And just because she made this one decision today didn't mean she couldn't still come back to Dan in a year and pick up where they left off, right? She owed it to herself to at least give it a try.

"Taylor, I'll see you at graduation, okay?" she said, standing up and heading for the door. She could already hear her family approaching.

"Uh, okay," said Taylor.

She probably said goodbye or something else as Joey opened the door and walked out, but her words fell away as Joey rejoined her family and encouraged them to pick up the pace.

She had a new graduation speech to write.

*

AS JOEY POSED for pictures with friends before the ceremony, she felt herself go through the motions. These pictures had been sitting in an album in her house for years and she knew how adorable she looked in them all. Except the one with that girl from her book club, Lori. Her eyes had been a bit too squinty in that one, so she made an effort to keep them open this time around.

"I'm really going to miss you," Lori said, pulling her into a hug.

Joey laughed, remembering how emotional and dramatic everything had seemed the first time she'd lived this day. Even Lori, who she didn't know all that well and was pretty sure she'd never see again, was hugging her longer than usual.

"Hey, can we maybe hang out some time this week?" Lori asked as the band began to play *Pomp and Circumstance*, their cue to line up.

"Oh, uh, sure," Joey said, feeling bad because she knew it was a lie. It occurred to her she'd probably also said yes the first time around, then forgotten in the hubbub of everything that came later that night. Lori always seemed so nice, and she'd blown her off then and was apparently going to do it again. Oops.

As she walked through the processional, she deliberately did not search the stands for Dan. She had a sneaking suspicion she'd never be able to go through with her plan if she saw him. And at this moment, her conviction to go through with it was teetering precariously, so best not to risk it.

The ceremony went just as she remembered it and she reached into the pocket of her robe to find her new, handwritten speech folded up, ready to be unleashed onto the unsuspecting crowd. Well, onto about ten people who would actually care, but same thing.

She looked up at the desert sky and smiled at the few stars she could see. It had felt so important to her in the following years that Dan had proposed under the stars. Now, they would be witness to her bravest moment.

As the principal announced her as valedictorian, she stood and made her way to the lectern, pulled out that piece of paper, and laughed as Betty yelled, "Joey's hot" from the stands, an inside sister joke they used to embarrass the other whenever possible.

"Faculty, family members, fellow graduates: we did it. We finished this chapter of our young lives and even though this feels like an ending, I know it's actually a beginning. This is the beginning of our lives as adults and our chance to make our own decisions. I know so many of us are hoping to succeed, but I am hoping we all fail."

Joey took a deep breath and allowed a confused laughter to reach her on the stage.

"That might sound funny, but it is with our failures that we learn the most. It is with our failures that we begin to appreciate success even more. Our failures make us human; make us better people. We hold our family and friends to more reasonable standards because we can give them the grace we also need, something we can only understand if we screw up every once in a while. And to truly love someone is to let them fail, love them anyway, and maybe even love them even more because of who they are and how they've failed you."

Joey again steadied herself and smiled as she looked at her next paragraph, wondering if anyone who read *Twilight* in the coming years would look back on her speech and think how similar they were, but also preparing herself to deliver a very important message to one person in particular.

"Now isn't the time to be sure of what we want to be in life. People have been asking us since we were little what we wanted to be when we grow up, but what eighteen-year-old knows the answer to that? Now is the time to go and try new things. Give one dream a try and if you fall on your face, go try another. You are young and limited only by the circumstances you choose to accept. And for anyone out there who is in a hurry to settle down when we should be anything but settled, I hope you find the patience and trust in your heart to know that asking someone else to abandon their dreams was never the right thing to do."

Joey finally let herself find Dan, seated in the front row of the bleachers. He looked confused, and maybe hurt, but she'd gone too far to stop now. And besides, she was too angry with him to even consider having this conversation one on one. She finished her speech, thanking her family and friends for supporting her through her years of school, but leaving out her special thanks to Dan she'd originally included. One way or another, he'd gotten his own, personal message.

As she walked back to her seat, she locked eyes with Taylor Page, who seemed to be asking her a question with her expression. Joey pictured the packed suitcase in her car, reminded herself it was only a year, then winked at Taylor before sitting back down for the rest of the ceremony.

As the last name was called and caps were thrown into the air, Joey put the final part of her plan into motion. Pushing her way through the crowd, she walked straight to Taylor and grabbed her hand. Not caring that any number of kids could be looking their way, she kissed her, then whispered, "Ready to run?" in her ear.

"I thought you'd never ask," Taylor said, before the two of them took off toward the parking lot, and all the beautiful question marks.

CHAPTER EIGHT

AS JOEY AND Taylor sat in the backseat of Taylor's parents' car, Joey tried to not picture her family reading the notes she'd left them in the bag she'd left with Betty to hold. It included her car keys and instructions for Betty to keep the car until she came home, along with letters for each of them with her best explanation on where she was going and why she had to do it.

She knew on a certain level it was still the end of an era, her childhood, whether she got engaged to Dan that night or took off for London, but there was something so much more final about putting thousands of miles between them with no warning. If she stopped to think about it, she never could have done it, so she instead looked to her left and sighed.

Taylor was shocked by the turn of events, but also the kind of person to not ask too many questions. Joey was especially appreciative of the second trait as they rode to Sky Harbor Airport. Apparently, Taylor's parents were also unperturbed by the change of plans and didn't question at all that Taylor's friend needed a ride to the airport as well. It put Taylor's shyness into full relief and Joey felt like she understood her so much better already. Growing up in a quiet house would probably make anyone pretty quiet.

As they pulled up to the departures level of Terminal Four, they didn't even question why Joey had so few bags. For Joey, someone who overthought everything and always packed carefully, it was unnerving to realize she hadn't even made a list of what to bring, but since she was trying out a new life, she thought a new "just go with it" attitude was worth also trying out.

Joey stood awkwardly as Taylor hugged her parents goodbye and choked back tears, failing miserably at shutting out the images of her family, Dan, and Dan's family, all standing there without her. She knew if she'd gotten near them, she wouldn't have been able to escape without explaining, and how could she explain? Making up her mind alone in her room had been one thing, but under the eyes of her closest family and friends, she knew she'd take the easier, well-known path.

As Taylor's parents pulled away, she turned to look at Joey with tears in her eyes.

"You know, it's weird," she said. "I've been so scared to leave and thought I'd have some big breakdown when they drove away, but now you're here with me..."

Joey used the back of her hand to wipe away her own tears and smiled. "I know what you mean. I think I'd be sobbing if it weren't for you."

"It's like camp." Taylor picked up her backpack and adjusted the rest of her bags as they began to walk into the terminal.

Joey blushed, remembering their last night in the dorm and wondering how they'd gotten to that topic so quickly, before Taylor continued, "I was so scared when they dropped me off, but you were there and I felt brave."

"I didn't know you were nervous," Joey said. "You always seemed so happy."

They lined up behind a few other travelers to check their luggage and stood quietly for a minute, realizing these weren't the kinds of conversations to have within earshot of strangers. But as she stood, Joey thought back on her memories with Taylor and realized she did seem to be more at ease whenever Joey was around. Maybe coming back to this date would be just as important to Taylor as it was for her.

After they dropped off their bags, Joey reached down to check her phone. She'd turned it to silent during the ceremony and purposely not checked it since they left. She had even considered leaving it behind, since she was pretty sure it wouldn't work in London anyway, but as she didn't have most phone numbers memorized other than her own house, she thought she should keep it with her.

Twenty-seven missed calls.

That seemed about right. Taylor noticed her looking at it and said, "So, did you tell anyone you were doing this?"

"Nope," Joey said. "I left them letters, but knew they'd try to talk me out of it if I said it out loud."

As they made their way up the escalators toward security, Joey's finger hovered over her voicemail button.

"Maybe wait until we get there?" Taylor said, looking down at her hand. "I can ask my mom to call your mom when we arrive so they know you're safe."

Joey felt like a coward, but knew Taylor was right. Emotional messages might be enough to talk her out of getting on the plane and she was still pretty sure she wanted to leave. Probably at least 87 percent sure.

"Hey, so, where are you planning to stay when we get there?" Taylor asked as they waited with the rest of the travelers to have their bags and bodies scanned.

Joey was called up by the TSA agent at that exact moment, and she tried not to seem too panicked as it occurred to her that she was about twelve hours away from arriving in a strange city with no place to live. She handed over her passport and took what she hoped was a "don't worry, I'm not a threat" deep breath. The agent seemed to think she was okay and sent her on her way, but now Joey thought it wasn't just the cellphone full of messages that would keep her from boarding.

She had money saved up from babysitting and other jobs through the years, but London was one of the most expensive cities in the world. She knew she could talk to the school about her scholarship and hopefully still use it for tuition, room, and board, but the first day of school was over three months away. Leaving on graduation night suddenly felt reckless and stupid. Why couldn't she have just turned Dan down tonight and left in September?

"I mean, my room is probably really small, but you're welcome to crash for a bit if you want," Taylor was saying as she caught up to her at the X-ray machines.

"Wait, what?" Joey said, as she reached down to pull her purse from the conveyer belt, nearly falling over from losing her balance as she yanked it a bit too hard. Or maybe it was from shock and relief.

"Oh, I mean, you don't have to," Taylor said. "But it's a single and I've got the room until classes start. It'll be like camp!"

Now it was Taylor's turn to blush and Joey realized the weight of her offer was hitting them both. Crashing with a friend was one thing, but suddenly living with someone who you had feelings for was a monumental step in a relationship. Or friendship. Joey was perhaps again over-thinking things, but could she call this a relationship? Taylor didn't know that Joey was walking away from a proposal that night and it would be extremely unfair to put that kind of pressure on something so new.

They walked again in silence after collecting the rest of their bags. As annoying as the new airport restrictions were since everything that had happened last September, Joey was suddenly relieved for one new security measure. Dan couldn't come chase her down at the airport without a ticket, and she was pretty sure he wouldn't buy one. Had she tried to leave abruptly last year, she was certainly facing a dramatic *Love Actually* moment.

Oh, hey, has that come out yet? she wondered as they walked to their gate.

They found two seats together and sat down with their bags placed in front of them.

"I'd love to crash with you, if you're sure you don't mind," Joey said, breaking the silence at last.

"Oh, great!" Taylor said. "I think this could be the best summer ever."

Joey took stock of where her life was heading, versus where it had the last time she'd lived this day. She looked down at her left hand where her engagement ring should be. A ring that was probably still in Dan's pocket, if he hadn't thrown it in the trash by now. If they were meant to be, maybe she'd be back in a year and ready to say yes to him, assuming he still wanted her.

And assuming she still wanted him, for that matter. As the flight attendant called for early boarding, Joey looked at Taylor and reminded herself that Dan had tried to keep her from following her dream. That betrayal and how distant he'd become in their other timeline felt like the perfect bookends to their story. In keeping her from her dream at eighteen, had he accidentally turned her into a thirty-eight-year-old woman whom he no longer loved?

That thought made boarding the plane easier than she thought it would be. If she could just alter their timeline enough to ease any resentment between them, maybe they'd both end up happy in the end, no matter who they married.

Or maybe she'd just ruined both of their lives and erased her three perfect children from existence.

As the flight attendants closed the doors, she hoped with all her might it was the former.

Chapter Nine

JOEY AND TAYLOR spent the flight chatting quietly about anything and everything. It would have been smart to sleep, but Joey remembered with a laugh that she was eighteen again and was pretty sure jetlag wouldn't hurt her teenage body the way it did her adult one. She found herself nervous at one point wondering how she'd pass the time without a smartphone, but three hours went by before she and Taylor realized other passengers were trying to sleep and decided to be quiet out of respect.

Joey walked to the back of the plane and bought two pair of headphones from a flight attendant so they could plug in to watch the in-flight movie. It was *A Walk to Remember,* and Joey tried to not remember dragging Dan to see it with her. He'd been so sweet and held her hand as she cried through the end, then told her on the drive home that he couldn't wait to marry her. She'd known he'd felt that way for years and loved how easily he could talk about their future.

Joey felt Taylor's head on her shoulder and knew she was asleep or close to it, so she tried to focus on the movie to keep her memories at bay. But as the plane carried them both further and further from home, Joey could almost feel her world shifting.

Shortly after he'd proposed, Dan had taken her to Tempe to show her the apartment he'd picked out for them. It was small, with two bedrooms, but it was all theirs and they had reveled in the feeling of actually being able to start their lives together. After scrounging together some furniture odds and ends and packing up their rooms, they had spent their first night at the apartment about a week after their graduations.

Joey smiled at the memory. Dan had insisted that he go in first and left her waiting outside the door for a few minutes. Just as she was getting annoyed, she heard music playing and Dan opened the door with a big, goofy grin.

"Welcome home, my love," he said, scooping her up into a bear hug and kissing her deeply. She noticed he'd turned on "Wouldn't It Be Nice" by the Beach Boys, one of their favorite songs. The one they'd listen to and dream about the day when they could spend the day together then hold each other close the whole night through. He'd put her back down but then picked her back up again, and this time he'd carried her across the threshold.

When he put her down again, she looked into their tiny living room to see a picnic candlelight dinner set up, which was both adorable and necessary, as they hadn't found a dining room table just yet. It was all so sweet, and she had wondered then how the night could be any more perfect, or her life for that matter.

"I'm glad we don't have any furniture yet," she had said as they finished the sandwiches Dan had prepared and brought with him for their first meal in their new home.

"Well, we do have *some* furniture," he said, nodding toward the bedroom. Their bedroom. It would be an adjustment to think of a room as theirs, and not hers.

"Indeed, we do, Mr. Shaw."

"Shall we go test out said furniture, soon-to-be-Mrs.-Shaw?" Dan raised his eyebrows flirtatiously.

"Well, seeing as how it's only seven o'clock, that seems a bit early to be heading to bed," Joey said, laughing. "Or are we pretending to be an old married couple already?"

"Maybe not an old one." Dan took her hand. "But I did wonder if you might want to do things that married couples do?"

Joey caught on to his train of thought finally and took a second to think. They'd been together for years and had managed to save one last act for marriage. He'd never really pressured her, and she'd never really officially said she didn't want to, but that maybe they should just wait? Sure, they'd been close, and they'd even talked about doing it as prom came around, but then she'd decided that was too trite.

It wasn't that she didn't feel ready for sex. It was more she had goals to focus on and sex could lead to babies. She knew there were ways to prevent it, but nothing was as tried and true as good old abstinence. She'd gone on birth control earlier that year to help regulate her cycle and lessen some of her monthly symptoms, but there were other advantages to waiting, chief among them not being walked in on by parents or siblings.

But now? They lived together. They'd share a bed every night. She was his and he was hers and she knew that was how it would always be. She did want to be together in that way, after all.

And so, she stood up first and reached down to take his hand, then led him to their bedroom.

"Are you sure?" he said. "Only if you're ready."

She looked at the bed and looked at Dan. She was thrilled they had waited as long as they did because suddenly this felt like the perfect time.

"I'm sure," she said, before kissing him.

"Hang on." He ran back to the other room.

She heard the music change and laughed as he came back in, holding the two candles he'd set out for their dinner.

"Did you make a sex music CD?" she asked as he put the candles down on the nightstand, which was the only piece of furniture in the room besides the bed.

"About a year ago," he said shyly. "Just wanted to be ready in case it came up."

She laughed and realized in that moment how much she loved him. He'd been hoping for this moment for ages, but never once pressured her. But, in his own sweet, Dan way, he'd been ready to make it special for her. He came back to her and kissed her gently as they made their way to the bed and were finally together in a way they hadn't been before.

That had always been one of her favorite memories, but now it felt so tainted by the sting of Dan's betrayal with the letter. If he really loved her, couldn't he have let her go to London to hone her craft before settling down together? Or at least decided against that herself?

She'd wanted to be a writer her whole life and he knew it, but as newspapers began to close while they were in school, he'd encouraged her to change majors to something more practical. Or had it been her idea?

"You can always write later," he said. And she knew he was right on some level, but with a day job, then one kid after another, her writing got pushed back further and further. And she'd been the one who wanted to stay home with the kids, so it made sense for him to keep going with his career while she fell a bit behind. That certainly wasn't his fault, but she'd blinked and twenty years had gone by, with only unfinished manuscripts to show for it.

That's not all you have to show for those twenty years, she reminded herself. She certainly was good at arguing both sides of an issue inside her head, an understandable result of being captain of the debate team for three years.

Somewhere over the Atlantic, she stopped going in circles about whether it had been she or Dan who had been the catalyst for her to stop writing and drifted off to sleep. And maybe it was her subconscious, or the beginning of a dream, but she felt herself realize at some point that she was now free to write as much as she'd like.

And oh, did she have stories to tell.

CHAPTER TEN

AS THE CABIN lights turned back on and passengers began opening their window blinds, Joey woke up and realized they'd shifted positions at some point, and she had fallen asleep on Taylor's shoulder. It was almost as jarring as waking up in her high school bedroom the day before, as she opened her eyes and found herself looking straight down Taylor's shirt and directly at her cleavage. Taylor hadn't stirred yet, so she gave herself a minute to fantasize about things that might be coming up for them.

Ever since the night they'd kissed, Joey had known she was bisexual. There didn't seem to be any point in discussing it with anyone as she continued with her relationship with Dan, but it was just something she knew about herself, but never acknowledged.

She was equally attracted to both sexes. So what? If she wasn't going to act on it, did it even mean anything?

As she looked down upon Taylor, though, she realized it definitely did mean something, in this timeline anyway. She'd been the one to help Taylor realize she was gay. Could Taylor be the one to help her finally, fully acknowledge her own status? Maybe these feelings weren't what she thought they were. What if she and Taylor did stuff and she realized those feelings were just curiosity? She'd always been happy with Dan in that way. Could she be equally happy with a woman?

As Taylor cleared her throat, Joey bolted upright and realized she hadn't been as subtle as she'd thought. Taylor was smiling her sweet, shy smile, but there was something else in her eyes. Amusement? She looked like she might laugh.

"See anything you like?" she whispered, leaning forward suggestively.

Flirting. She was flirting with Joey and the look in her eyes was more like excitement than anything else. Maybe even lust.

The time for being coy and chatting as friends was over, Joey decided. She glanced over her shoulder to check that their seatmate was still asleep, then leaned over to kiss Taylor, gently. The same sparks they'd had all those years ago were most definitely still there and Joey knew in an instant that she absolutely could be attracted to members of both sexes, or at least to Dan and Taylor simultaneously.

The flight attendants came around with breakfast biscuits as their seatmate woke up, so Joey settled back into her seat and gave Taylor's hand a squeeze as they waited for their snacks and juice. Joey was sure she couldn't be any happier than she was in that moment, until Taylor squeezed her hand back and her stomach flipped. They sat there holding hands until the woman sitting next to them coughed pointedly and she remembered that being out in 2002 was very different from the world she'd left behind. Not that it was necessarily easy for her gay friends in 2022, but she realized with a pang that same-sex marriage wouldn't be legal for another thirteen years in the States.

As much as she had supported LGBTQ causes in her life with Dan, she'd never fully let herself think about what it was like to be in that community, nor acknowledge that she was, on some level. As she let go of Taylor's hand, she tried to remember what year the UK had allowed gay couples to marry and was annoyed that all she could remember was that it was slightly before the US did. If she did end up with Taylor, what kind of life would await them?

Her thoughts made her juice taste bitter, so she again tried to focus back on the here and now. They were making their final approach in London, and she had a place to stay. That was good. She had some money saved, also good. She also knew enough about things that were coming up that she could maybe turn her savings into something more substantial. Was that too Biff in *Back to the Future II*? Or just using the random trivia in her head to her advantage?

She scanned her brain for stats that might come in handy. The Diamondbacks won the World Series in 2001, but who won in 2002?

The Angels, she said to herself. The answer came to her quickly, but she wasn't sure how sure she actually was. And even if she was sure, was betting her life savings on the outcome of a sporting event a wise move? What if coming back to this year had screwed up something in the space-time continuum and the Angels no longer won?

Okay, so she was sure they won in 2002. And since it was only May, she could probably get good odds if she placed her bet before the season was even halfway over. If she was going back to a time that wouldn't accept her relationship with Taylor, the least the universe could to was let her use the trivia she'd built up over the years to her advantage.

This logic made no sense, and she knew it, but the first decade of the new millennium had been so full of financial stress for her and Dan she thought how great it would be if she could eliminate that issue. What if she went back home a year from now with a few manuscripts under her belt and a nest egg for the two of them? If what she knew of Taylor was correct, she wouldn't even meet her eventual partner for a few years, so she wouldn't screw that up for her if things didn't work out between the two of them.

Finally, she felt fully at ease with her decision. As she and

Taylor exited the plane at Heathrow, Joey told herself she needed to stop thinking of every moment in terms of a lifetime. All she had to do was live each of these new moments and let things fall into place.

She followed Taylor to a bank of payphones, resisting the urge to comment that she hadn't seen one in years. Taylor pulled out a calling card and again Joey had to stifle a gasp at the blast from the past.

"Hey, Mom," Taylor said, a little too loudly. Joey had forgotten that international calls used to be a big deal and connections were often spotty. "Yeah, we just landed. Everything's fine, but could you call Joey's mom and let her know we're fine and that Joey will call her soon? We just need to get her a phone or a calling card, I'm almost out of minutes on this."

Taylor paused to let her mom answer, then quickly dictated Joey's home phone number. It was nice of Mrs. Page to make the call for her, but she didn't envy her that task. Her mom must be so hurt.

Or was she? Of all the family members on both sides, her mom had always been the one who seemed to imply she might be rushing into things. She loved Dan, to be sure, but didn't see the need for them to get married at nineteen. However, she'd trusted her daughter and didn't belabor the point when it was clear that Joey had made up her mind. Nor did she complain about becoming a grandmother at fifty, fifty-two, and fifty-four. Any reservations she'd had about her daughter marrying young went right out of the window the moment she held her first grandchild and she loved nothing more than getting down on the floor to play with them.

But still, Joey couldn't help but wonder if her mom might give a little cheer upon reading her letter from last night. Her dad might even be excited for her. And though it was unlikely, she could even see Betty coming around and being excited that her boring, predictable older sister had finally shown some gumption.

As Taylor finished her call, Joey looked around the airport and let the full reality sink in. She was on another continent, ready to answer the ultimate "what might have been" questions that had rolled around her head for years.

She grabbed Taylor's hand as they walked to customs, neither noticing nor caring if anyone shot them dirty looks. It wouldn't be long until they were safely alone in Taylor's dorm room, and the possibilities awaiting them there were too exciting to allow anything other than happiness to register.

Chapter Eleven

A FEW TRAIN rides and some wrong turns later and they found themselves at the entrance to the London School of the Arts, which housed both Taylor's music conservatory and Joey's writing program. It was an old, beautiful school, made of brick and covered in greenery. Joey pictured herself sitting in a Starbucks back home, trying desperately to push past writer's block before she had to get home to relieve a babysitter. Writing here, she realized, would be a piece of cake and she couldn't wait to get started.

But first, they needed to drop their bags off in Taylor's room, which they quickly found thanks to the map the school had sent along with her orientation packet. The door was unlocked, and they both laughed as they opened it. The room was comically small. It had just enough room for a twin bed and small desk with a chair, and that was about it.

"You sure about that offer to have me crash here?" Joey said as they closed the door behind them. There was barely room for the two of them to stand in the middle of the room with their bags nearby. What would happen when they unpacked?

"Very sure," Taylor said. "We'll just spend most of our time outside. All we really have to do is sleep in here."

The word sleep made them both look at the tiny bed and blush.

"Hey, where's your cello?" Joey said, realizing Taylor seemed to have not packed a crucial piece of equipment.

"Oh, well, my parents bought me one here, as a graduation present." She cast her eyes down.

"That's awesome! Really, Taylor, that's such a nice gift."

Taylor exhaled and Joey knew why. As an only child, Taylor had been what some people might call spoiled. She got a brand-new car on her sixteenth birthday and her parents had been able to afford things other kids at their school could only dream of, like attending this school. Even before her scholarship, Taylor knew she'd be able to go, but she never flaunted any of it, so Joey didn't mind. Owning two cellos was obviously a luxury, but it made sense. Carting one back and forth internationally was not only a pain, but probably a little risky. And since Joey knew Taylor was going to make it in Europe as a musician, she was secretly impressed with the foresight of Mr. and Mrs. Page.

"Well, if you can store it somewhere else and use the practice rooms, I think you're right about this room," Joey said. "We'll be just fine."

She collapsed on the bed in a heap, suddenly aware of how tired she was.

"Not so fast," Taylor said, reaching down to pull her up. "We can't go to sleep yet. We have to try and stay awake and adjust to this time zone."

Joey resisted and pulled Taylor gently down to the bed with her.

"Okay, so no sleep," Joey said. "I can think of other things we can do in this bed."

Taylor smiled and leaned forward to kiss Joey as they both adjusted themselves so they were soon completely horizontal and facing each other on the bed. Joey realized it wasn't as small as it looked as they both fit comfortably. And besides, being right up against Taylor each night seemed like a pretty good thing.

They kissed and kissed some more, and Joey recognized that old feeling of being in a space of her own with someone she cared about for the first time. She might have the memories of a thirty-eight-year-old, but clearly had the hormones of an eighteen-year-old and she was nearly overwhelmed with how strong her emotions were in that moment.

She wondered if she ought to pump the brakes a bit but

decided to let Taylor take the lead. She wanted to know her better to see if Mary Fate had been right, but that certainly didn't just mean physical stuff, nor did it mean they had to do all the things on their first day together.

As they kissed, Taylor's hands explored Joey's body and Joey answered each touch with one of her own, taking her cues as she went. She wondered why anyone felt the need to label another person's sexual preferences as she went; wasn't a body just a body? Why did it matter that she and Taylor had the same parts?

But in the same way she knew that it didn't matter to her, she knew it mattered quite a bit to a lot of people and tried to push those thoughts from her mind. Heck, it even mattered to the person whose body she was currently exploring. Taylor had known from a young age that she just didn't feel anything when she kissed a boy. And not just any boy, but Johnny Sanglin, widely acknowledged as the hottest guy in their school.

Joey felt oddly proud and sexy that she'd been someone Taylor had been attracted to over Johnny. It wasn't a competition and certainly not fair since Taylor wasn't attracted to men in general, but still: Taylor had chosen her then and was choosing her again now.

"Have you ever been with a woman?" Taylor asked, pulling Joey back into the moment.

"Not since you and I kissed." Joey took the opportunity to catch her breath.

"I meant have you had sex, but I'll take that as a no." Taylor laughed.

"Ah, no," Joey said, also laughing. "I've never had sex."

"At all?" Taylor sounded surprised. "I thought you and Dan...?"

"Not until next week." Joey realized a moment too late that her reply made no sense. "I mean year. We were thinking we'd wait until next year."

"Oh. And here I thought I was at risk of comparison."

"Well, we've done other things. But not all the way."

"So, we can be each other's firsts," Taylor said matter-of-factly. "I like that."

Taylor leaned forward to kiss Joey again and picked up where she'd left off with her hands. As much as Joey didn't want to stop, she tried to put herself back into the mindset of an eighteen-year-old and knew they should probably slow things down before things went too far. She gently took Taylor's hands in her own and brought them up to her lips to kiss them.

"Hey, we're in London," she said. "What do you say we go explore the city for a bit?"

Taylor flinched, but then nodded.

"Trust me, I want to keep going." Joey pulled Taylor's chin up a bit before kissing her again. "But we have time. And a very small bed. I have a feeling we're going to know each other's bodies very well by the time this summer's over."

Taylor laughed and pushed herself up into a sitting position. Her hair was a mess after the long flight and subsequent fooling around, and Joey realized she was likely similarly disheveled.

After a quick stop by the community loo, they left the room for their first official outing as a couple. Even though Joey was eager to get back to bed, she was equally eager to get to know Taylor and their new home. And besides, she was right; they had nothing but time.

CHAPTER TWELVE

THE FUNNY THING about the best laid plans is that they oft get really messed up. That's not how the saying goes, but it was as close as Joey could get after she and Taylor found a nearby pub and realized the drinking age is only eighteen in the UK.

Their intentions had been good; really, they had. After walking around for a while, they quickly realized they needed some sort of map. And even though they wanted to play tourist, neither had remembered to bring a camera. So, they walked back toward the school until Taylor had the brilliant idea to inquire inside the pub about where they might find a map or directions for when they were ready to go back out.

But when the bartender asked what they wanted and it dawned

on them both that they could actually order a drink, those best laid plans went right out of the window. Joey didn't know much about beer, having always stuck to wine and mixed drinks, but she remembered liking cider, so they each ordered a pint and found an open table near a rather loud group of rugby players. After just a few sips, they were both feeling pretty tipsy. Jetlag, low tolerance for alcohol, and being literal lightweights made for quite the combination.

"I bet the rugby boys behind us know where to find a map," Joey said, feeling very smart and bold.

"Maybe they even have a map," Taylor said. They were both already coming up with the best ideas.

And so, they joined the rugby team and got all kinds of advice on places to go and things to do. Joey knew the guys were hitting on Taylor, who was gorgeous even after a day of air travel, and maybe even a bit with her, too, seeing as how she was eighteen and things were all pointing up again. They weren't aggressive or anything, and Joey was thankful for British chivalry as they finished their pints.

"Let us buy you another round," one of them said, clearly sad to see them go.

"Another time, lads," Taylor said. Joey was amazed at how she handled herself around these strangers, but suspected the beer had something to do with it.

"Yeah, thanks for all the great advice," Joey added. Whereas that might have led to guys back home protesting or calling them both teases or worse, here, it simply signaled the end of their conversation.

"We'll see you around," another one of the rugby boys said. "We're here after all our games. Maybe you both could come watch us play sometimes. Tuesdays and Thursdays? Just around the corner from your college."

"Sounds great," Joey said as they stood to leave. Taylor nodded and gave Joey an urgent look as they made their way to the door.

"What's wrong?" Joey asked as they got outside.

"Oh nothing," Taylor said. "I just wanted to do this."

Taylor gently guided Joey up against the wall of the pub and kissed her. Joey could taste the cider on her tongue and liked how the whole moment made her tingle. Or maybe it was the alcohol coursing through her veins.

"Those boys were hitting on you," Taylor said. "It was cute."

"Nah, they were hitting on you," Joey replied. "And I don't blame them."

Taylor kissed her again and grabbed her hand as they walked back to the dorm. Behind them, they heard the door of the pub open and out walked two of their new friends. Taylor raised her hand to wave just as the two of them began to kiss, right where Taylor and Joey had just been.

"Ahh," laughed Joey. "Maybe they weren't hitting on either of us."

"Ha! Maybe we're just not used to guys talking to us just to talk to us. This is kinda nice."

"I agree." Joey tripped a bit on the sidewalk before Taylor steadied her. "I might have been wrong about them, but this is me hitting on you: you're the most beautiful girl I've ever known."

Taylor squeezed her hand and on they walked, smiling and swinging their arms together with the rhythm of their steps. The sun hadn't quite set, but Joey was glad they'd at least killed some time. They could go out and explore after getting a good night's sleep. The air was cool and crisp, which was waking her back up a bit after the warmth of the pub combined with the cider, but she knew it wouldn't take long to fall asleep once she tried.

But as they walked back into the dorm room, Joey looked again at the bed and back at Taylor, who was locking the door behind them.

"Are you sleepy?" she asked, once again prepared to let Taylor take the lead.

Taylor looked her in the eye, kicked off her shoes, dropped her sweater on the floor, and pulled her shirt up over her head. As Joey took in the sight of Taylor's perfect body in just her bra and jeans, her sleepy brain woke right back up.

"Are you drunk?" Joey asked.

"Tipsy," Taylor said. "But everything I'm thinking is exactly what I was thinking before we left. I've dreamed of this since camp. I always hoped it would be with you, but never thought we'd actually get here."

Joey took off her clothes until she was down to her bra and underwear, raising the ante ever so slightly. She didn't want to pressure Taylor, but she was also kinda hot after the walk and her jeans felt like they were completely stuck to her skin. Maybe she'd think more clearly with them off.

That might have worked, but Taylor seemed to take it as a challenge and called her raise.

"Truth or dare?" she said as she tossed her jeans into a pile along with the rest of her clothes.

"Truth," said Joey.

"Are you still in love with Dan?"

"Yes. But I don't want to be."

"I can live with that."

"Truth or dare?" Joey said.

"Dare," Taylor replied.

Joey raised an eyebrow and pointed to the bed. Taylor turned out the light, grabbed her hand, and as they laid down together, Joey whispered her dare into the darkness.

And Taylor, apparently never one to back down from a dare, obliged.

CHAPTER THIRTEEN

JUNE BROUGHT SUNSHINE and warmer weather to London, turning the city into the perfect place for two young girls in love. It took about a month, but Joey and Taylor began to hit their stride, even being mistaken for locals from time to time.

As they sat with their rugby friends at the local pub again one Tuesday afternoon, Joey felt a tap on her shoulder.

"Excuse me," said the woman, clearly American. "Can you tell us how to find the closest subway station?"

Joey smiled and asked the woman and her friend where they were from (Colorado). They swapped stories about how they'd both come to be so far from home, then Joey gave her instructions on how to find her way back to her hotel, along with some tips on things to do while she was there.

"Did you hear that?" she said, rejoining the group. "She thinks I'm a Londoner!"

"Nah, she just thought you were the most approachable," said Taylor. "We're surrounded by sweaty men, and I accidently scowled at her when she came in."

"Why would you do that?"

"I wasn't scowling *at* her." Taylor put her hands up defensively. "I was trying to do math, and she walked right into my long division scowl."

They both laughed and Joey kissed Taylor on the nose. "Still trying to split the tab?"

Taylor nodded and sighed. Meeting the guys after rugby had become a routine and they always insisted on picking up the tab, but that never stopped Taylor from trying to slip money into their pockets to pay their share. Joey had picked up a part-time job at the school after officially registering and accepting her scholarship, but the guys could tell money was tight for the two of them and since they enjoyed having them around and could afford it, a pattern had emerged.

Joey thought it was sweet, but Taylor still hadn't come around on the idea. Actually, she had been fine with it until the wedding.

Liam and Will, the two they'd seen kissing on their first night in London, were a couple, but not out to their families. About two weeks after Joey and Taylor met them, the boys asked if they could take them to a wedding they were set to be groomsmen in, as dates. Taylor was hesitant, but Joey jumped at the chance to attend a British wedding, eventually convincing Taylor it would be fun.

And it was. They all had a great time, dancing the night away, until one of the guests called Liam a poof. Worried it might come to blows or at least lead to an extremely awkward situation, Joey had stepped in and kissed Liam, long enough for the other guy to shrug and walk away.

Taylor wasn't mad. She was proud of Joey for helping their friend like that but said the only weird thing was letting them buy their drinks going forward.

"It feels like prostitution," she said one night, back in the dorm.

"If kissing a friend to protect him in exchange for some drinks makes me a hooker, then call me Pretty Woman, I guess," Joey laughed. "Although, the one thing she wouldn't do was kiss on the mouth."

They'd both laughed and Joey hoped that would end it, but there was still the teensiest tension under the surface. Luckily, it faded as time went on, and soon Taylor, Joey, Will, and Liam were quite the foursome, seeing plays together, meeting to read in the park, gathering for Sunday brunch. On the days when Taylor was in long rehearsals and Joey had a free afternoon, she'd take her laptop over to their campus and write under a shady tree while the boys played rugby or did their summer homework.

Speaking of tension, Joey had managed a few awkward phone calls home, with mixed results. Her parents weren't upset with her choice but made it clear they just didn't appreciate how she left so abruptly (fair), nor how she'd treated Dan (extremely fair). Betty had initially refused to speak to her but softened that stance just before the one-month mark when she had a favor to ask.

"Okay, I'll forgive you," said Betty, with a dramatic sigh. "But on one condition."

"Okay?"

"You have to forgive me if I ever do something that hurts you. One free pass."

"Are you planning something? Because this feels premeditated."

"No, no plan. Just if it comes up. We'll call it even. Deal?"

"Well, yeah," said Joey. "Of course I'll forgive you."

Her call with Dan, on the other hand, was brutal. He never mentioned his plans to propose that night. She was hoping he would so she could allude to the fact she was still open to that possibility, down the road.

"If you'd told me about London, you know I would have supported you," he said.

If he was going to lie, she figured she might as well too.

"It was a last-minute decision," she said. "I just needed to be impulsive, for once in my life."

Well, that was a half-truth, anyway.

"Well, you impulsively broke my heart." Even though the connection was terrible, she could tell he was crying.

She wanted to say he'd broken hers as well, and he was going to do it again, years from now. He was going to pull away from her, leaving her feeling small and alone. Maybe this year apart was the reset button they needed to avoid that fate.

"I know. And I'm sorry," was all she could say.

Even though the calls hadn't gone perfectly, Joey felt lighter once the first round was done. It helped her focus solely on Taylor and their new life together. She couldn't shake the feeling that she could still just use this year as a way of fixing her original timeline, but the longer she was away, the easier it was to imagine being happy with either option.

You married the wrong person. She fell asleep most nights with that voice and those words ringing in her ears. It was so crazy to think it might be true, but wasn't everything about this situation crazy? The woman who said those words was somehow powerful enough to send her back in time twenty years.

Was she also powerful enough to predict the future?

Chapter Fourteen

LEANING INTO A timeline solely focused on Taylor turned out to be easier than Joey had imagined. The dorm room was cramped, and they soon had to share a bathroom with the rest of the summer students, but it's easy to be smooshed in next to someone all the time when you're falling in love.

And Joey was. Hard.

It wasn't just her physical attraction to Taylor, which was immense. They'd spent countless hours together now, learning how to make love and giggling with each new discovery. They were careful to not be too affectionate in public, lest they attract unwanted attention, but their room was their sanctuary, and they couldn't keep their hands off each other.

But more than that, it was their emotional connection. Joey was used to being in love with her best friend, and it was that kind of love she craved. Thus, the more they got to know each other, the deeper their friendship grew, and the more Joey questioned how she'd ever thought she could be happy anywhere else.

Will's family was from Cornwall, and since he was dying to bring Liam home on the weekends that summer, they once again asked Taylor and Joey to accompany them, posing as girlfriends.

"Just until we feel comfortable telling our parents," Will had pleaded.

Joey was sure Taylor would object, but she said yes before Joey even had tried to talk her into it.

"Are you sure?" Joey asked as they packed up to leave one Friday for their first weekend away.

"He wants to see his family," Taylor said softly. "And he wants them to know his boyfriend. I don't love the lying, but I get it. Maybe his parents will love Liam and we won't have to pretend for too long?"

Joey put down the clothes she'd been folding and pulled Taylor into her arms, then kissed her. As she stepped back, she looked her in the eyes and said, "That's why I love you, Taylor Page."

"Hey, you know something?" Taylor's cheeks burned red. "I kinda love you too!"

"Kinda?" said Joey with mock incredulity.

"Well, it's a bit more than kinda." Taylor stepped back to

continue packing. "It's more of a 'holy moly this is the best feeling ever' kind of love."

"That's better." Joey threw a pair of socks at Taylor playfully.

Try as she might, Joey couldn't help but flash back to when Dan had first told her those same words.

It was her sixteenth birthday. They'd been together for almost two years and had been saying "I love you" since they were kids. It was just something they said when they were more like siblings, so saying it as a couple had seemed so natural.

But on that night, after the rest of her party guests had gone home, Dan had taken her to her driveway to "say goodnight." This was usually code for one of their make-out sessions, but before the kissing could begin, Dan faced her and said, "I love you."

"I love you too," she said, still waiting to be kissed.

"No, I really love you," he said emphatically.

"So, you didn't really love me before?"

"No, I did. I just don't think I knew what it meant before. I don't mean I love you like it's something we're supposed to say at the end of the night. I love you like you're a part of me. I love you like I'd do anything to keep you safe. I love you like I don't know what I'd do if I ever lost you. I love you, for real."

From then on, they added those two words to the end of their exchanges, including in their wedding vows. Hearing two nineteen-year-olds say, "I love you for real," probably reinforced just how young they were to most of their guests, but it was the most grown-up thing they could have ever said.

Try as she might, she couldn't help but flash back to the months leading up to the reunion, when he'd stopped saying the words.

"Come on, you know I love you," he had said when she asked why he never told her that anymore.

"How? How do I know that?" she'd said, trying and failing to brush all the tears from her face. They wouldn't stop falling lately.

"Everything I do is to support you and this family." He'd raised his voice. "Why would I do that if I don't love you?"

"But do you love me for real?" She'd hoped to unlock a bit of their old magic.

"That's just something kids say," he'd said, then walked away.

Looking at Taylor, Joey searched her soul in this moment. Did she love Taylor for real? Yes, she certainly cared a great deal for her, but they were still in the infatuation stage, so it was hard to tell. She knew if she'd experienced this at eighteen for the first time, she definitely would have convinced herself it was for real. Was that how it had been with her and Dan?

Maybe she wasn't fully there yet, but she was certainly on her way.

And in two hours, she, Taylor, Will, and Liam were on their way to the coast, sharing a bottle of wine on the train to Cornwall. They were seated as two boy/girl couples, and Joey smiled as she played footsie with Taylor, who was seated across from her. Joey was there to be Liam's girlfriend and Taylor was there to be Will's. Will's family was pretty conservative, so even though they were happy to host the two couples, they did ask that the girls room together and the boys do the same.

The foursome laughed at the arrangement but promised to be on their best behavior.

"Trust me," said Will. "You're going to want to come home with me every weekend."

Joey couldn't imagine any place being worth having to hide her relationship every weekend, but when they arrived, she relaxed her scruples immediately. The house was gorgeous and overlooked the sea. They could ride bikes to the local markets and restaurants, sit on the beach for hours, and basically have holiday after holiday, all for the low price of pretending to be heterosexual.

But really, how bad was that? Down by the water and away from Will's family's view, they were free to do as they pleased. And even though they went to bed each night tipsy and giddy after drinking, neither couple broke any house rules.

At meals, they managed to appear like perfect college sweethearts. Will's parents loved Taylor and were already planning to come see her end of summer concert at the conservatory. But they also really seemed to like Liam, so Taylor's hope that their involvement might soften the eventual blow even felt like it could work.

As their first weekend there came to an end, Will's parents said they were welcome to come back any time.

"And I know you're trying to be respectful in front of your old mum," Will's dad said with a laugh, "but you shouldn't go so long without kissing that girl of yours."

He clapped his son on the back and nudged him toward Taylor. And even though it only lasted a few seconds, Joey couldn't help but feel a twinge of jealousy watching her girlfriend kiss someone else.

"You okay?" Taylor said as they got to the train station.

"Of course," Joey said, scanning her brain to make sure it was true.

As they took their seats, Will broke the tension at last by saying, "No offense, but that was like kissing my sister."

Joey felt the initial twinge fade away as the train took them back to London, but as she fell asleep that night, she wished it didn't have to be that way.

CHAPTER FIFTEEN

SUMMER FADED INTO fall as summers always do, and it was time for Joey to start her first college classes. Her biggest draw to this school was that she didn't have to take the normal prerequisite classes but could instead dive right into her writing program. She and Taylor had been assigned as roommates, so they moved from their tiny dorm room into a slightly less tiny room, with two beds, which they immediately pushed together.

Taylor had already made a name for herself at the music school and finished her initial program by performing a solo piece at the end of summer show. As promised, Will's parents had come up from Cornwall, and had even taken them all out to a fancy dinner.

Their weekends in Cornwall were some of the best of her life, and since she already felt lucky enough to be living two lifetimes, she worried she was somehow taking more than her fair share of joy. Because that was her main emotion: pure, radiant joy. Will's parents commented often about how she and Liam must be heading down the aisle soon because Joey was basically glowing all the time.

They weren't wrong about the glowing, but it was all for Taylor. Taylor, who walked her to work each day before heading to class. Taylor, who read her short stories and laughed in all the right places. Taylor, who sat up with her for hours when her brain wouldn't shut down, talking through plot issues and helping her brainstorm new book ideas.

As eager as she was to start her writing classes, she couldn't bear to wait and had already nearly completed several full manuscripts. Twenty years of stories she'd collected and filed under "someday" seemed to pour out of her as soon as she opened her laptop. She could write for hours unencumbered. If Taylor saw that she was in the zone, she'd quietly leave water and snacks nearby, and maybe gently kiss her on the head.

It wasn't fair to compare, but everything was just easier with Taylor. Granted, they'd been lucky to make it through the summer by sharing Taylor's school meal plan, but the World Series was only weeks away and Joey's bet from May was about to pay off big time. The guy she'd placed it with had laughed when she'd done it, but she knew he was probably getting more and more nervous as the Angels made their way through the play-offs.

Not having to worry about money made it that much easier to focus on her writing, leaving all her spare time for Taylor. They found coats and boots at a local secondhand shop and looked forward to keeping each other warm through their first fall and winter in a non-desert climate.

As they walked home in their new cold-weather attire, Joey filled Taylor in on her newest manuscript idea.

"It's another murder mystery, but I think I've got the perfect twist," she said, ready to blow Taylor's mind with her new idea involving vampires and werewolves. She didn't think of it so much as copying *Twilight*, but more putting her own spin on a story that hadn't been written yet. In this timeline.

"Why is everything you write so dark?" Taylor asked.

"Mysteries sell," Joey said, taken aback. "Isn't that the point?"

"Not for me. I'm not an artist to make money. I'm an artist because I want to put beautiful things into the world."

"So, my stories aren't beautiful?" Joey stopped in her tracks.

"No, no, sweetie." Taylor pulled them both to the edge of the sidewalk so that people could pass. "I just think you have more in you than death and gore. I want to read the stories that are in your heart. You're such a gifted writer and I know you can do any genre. If these are the stories that move you, keep going. I just think you can do more."

Joey was thankful to hear this feedback as a grown-up in a teenager's body, because she knew exactly how she would have reacted hearing this as a kid. She sometimes wondered which of them actually had lived an additional twenty years already, as Taylor constantly surprised her with her wisdom.

Thus, instead of crying and storming off, Joey guided them both back to the sidewalk to continue their walk home. And while she walked, she thought about what she'd just heard. Yes, she had stories she'd been thinking about for years, but they all felt too personal. Could she really put them down on paper? She wrote fiction, so there was always the option to shrug everything off and say it was just a character, but she knew the people who loved her would always hear her voice in her stories and pick out the parts that weren't make-believe.

It was a weird dichotomy. She could write stories about serial killers and no one thought she might actually be one. But could she write a story about a girl from Arizona without people assuming everything on the page was a confession?

"You're not talking," said Taylor after a few minutes of silence. "Contemplating what I said or mad about what I said."

"Contemplating," Joey said. "And thankful that you care enough to challenge me."

"The world needs your stories, Joey. Especially young girls at camp who aren't sure who they can talk to about liking girls instead of boys."

Joey squeezed Taylor's hand and knew she was right.

When they got home, Joey sat down in front of her computer with a renewed sense of purpose. Then immediately chickened out. Maybe she could hide her stories in the middle of her mysteries? Two police officers who solve grisly murders, but then realize they're in love? But what about the vampires and werewolves? She knew better than to stare at a blank screen. The words would come when it was their time to come.

She shut the computer and herself down for the night and opened one of her textbooks. She was supposed to read this chapter on plotting everything out ahead of time, but the words seemed to jumble on the page. Shouldn't writing be spontaneous? Planning felt forced and seemed to remove all the artistry from the process.

She looked over at Taylor, who was curled up on her side of the bed, reading a novel. Their journey together seemed to point to spontaneity over planning. She looked back at the chapter. Part of her wanted to bomb the assignment, in silent protest, but she knew her school-minded brain wouldn't allow that. And after all, part of this new timeline experiment was for her to learn all she could as a writer.

She grabbed a notepad and began to follow the model listed in the chapter. She took Taylor's advice and kept it to a story she knew, using a character dissection and plot map as directed by the textbook. She used the prompts to fill in about five chapters' worth of things for each person to do and started to hit her stride as Taylor turned out the light. She still preferred her method, but maybe a little planning could make her story even better.

As she joined Taylor in bed, she applied what she'd just learned to her future and smiled in her sleep as her character waited at the end of an aisle for Taylor. But somewhere in the dream, Dan showed up and screamed that she'd married the wrong person.

She woke up with a gasp around two a.m., vowing never to do homework so close to bedtime again.

CHAPTER SIXTEEN

THE ANGELS WON the World Series right on schedule and Joey gleefully collected her winnings from a very annoyed book-maker. With money in the bank and the knowledge that she could make similar wagers throughout the years, Joey got to work on her Christmas plans. She'd never been able to actually buy her loved ones nice gifts in years past, and it was so fun to pick things out.

She and Taylor had decided not to go home for the holidays, so she couldn't buy gifts and take them to Arizona, but she had fun choosing things online and shipping them to her house, with in-structions for everyone to open their gifts on Christmas. She even sent a watch to Dan. It was something she knew he wanted, or would say he wanted in years to come, and she hoped it could serve as both a peace offering and symbolic gesture. She hoped he'd open it and realize that maybe all they needed was time.

London was all dressed up for the season and she and Taylor spent as much time as they could wandering the streets and kissing under the twinkly lights. As beautiful as the city was, though, she wanted to plan something extra special for Taylor, Will, and Liam. Their summer weekends in Cornwall had been so special, and she thought what better way to say thanks than a trip to Paris for New Year's Eve? The boys were always asking Taylor to show off her French, which was pretty good after eight years of classes.

It was especially hard to be away from home on Thanksgiving in a country that didn't celebrate it, so Joey came up with the idea to make a full, traditional dinner for everyone to show the boys what it was like. Unfortunately, she forgot that they didn't have access to a kitchen, so she called their favorite Sunday brunch place and asked if they wouldn't mind serving turkey that Thursday. Bob, the owner, obliged, and even posted flyers announcing it as a fun event, in case any other locals wanted to try a real American Thanksgiving dinner.

And so, Joey, Taylor, Liam, and Will found themselves crowded together at a table meant for two on Thanksgiving, since apparently the entire neighborhood was excited to give the food a try. Bob had done his best, but nothing tasted quite right to Joey or Taylor. But hey, they were together and shared what they were thankful for, so at least it sort of felt like being at home. Kind of.

As the other three finished giving thanks, Joey was nearly bursting with excitement. Even though the trip she had planned was a Christmas present, she didn't want to wait that long to announce it, to make sure no one made other plans.

"And Joey," Liam said, "what are you thankful for? And why are you bouncing in your seat?"

"I'm thankful that we're all going to Paris for New Year's!" she nearly shouted.

"We're what?" Taylor said, appropriately gobsmacked.

"I booked us adjoining rooms at a really nice hotel, along with tickets to their fancy party! Merry Christmas!"

"Is this an American thing?" said Will. "Do you give out Christmas presents a month early back in the States?"

"Oh, er, no," Joey said. "I just wanted to make sure we all saved the date. Is that okay?"

"Okay?" said Liam. "It's incredible. Well done, you."

"Yes, of course," said Will. "That sounds amazing."

Taylor's shock finally wore off and she joined in the excitement. "To Paris!" she said, raising her glass for a toast.

The month between Thanksgiving and Christmas flew by as it always does, with school finals and holiday concerts jamming their schedules like never before. Taylor was booked solid through the month of December, performing in quartets, symphonies, and solo, usually with barely enough time to get herself and her cello to the next show in time. Joey became her roadie and had the packing-up process down to about ninety seconds. They'd also both gotten pretty good at lugging everything through tube stations and knew which ones to avoid by the time the last concert ended just after midnight on Christmas Eve.

They arrived back in their dorm room that night, exhausted and giddy. Taylor passed out almost immediately, still dressed in her concert attire. Before Joey could join her, though, she let herself think back on her first Christmas with Dan, in their tiny apartment.

They were elbow deep in wedding plans and had said no gifts, but each of them had tried to be sneaky and still get the other something small. After spending Christmas Eve with both of their families, they drove home late that night and searched the skies for Santa and his reindeer. It was something they'd done together since they were kids, and something they'd continue with their own kids, eventually.

They walked in the door and Dan put on the Christmas mix CD he'd made earlier in the month. Joey reached behind the couch and pulled out the small package she'd wrapped while he was in class one day, then laughed as he pulled a gift from the cupboard above the stove, which she couldn't reach.

"You first," she had said, smiling as Dan carefully unwrapped the small box she'd used. It wasn't much, but she'd made him an ornament cube, each side holding a picture of them together through the years. In her best handwriting, she'd written "Our First Christmas" on the top in magic marker. She laughed remembering how it faded a little bit every year. When she'd offered to write it again, Dan had simply said, "Leave it. We know what it says."

"I love it," he said, kissing her gently. "Now you."

She wasn't nearly as careful as he was, and ripped the paper open quickly, before oohing over the fancy box. She assumed it was an old gift box his mom had somewhere, but as she opened it, she found an actual charm bracelet.

"I got it in Denmark on my class trip last year," he said. "I couldn't afford any charms, but I thought we could add those as we go."

"So, this is why you didn't come home with anything for yourself?" she asked, as he fixed the clasp on her wrist.

"Indeed it is."

The memory was sweet, but she reached down to her empty right wrist and sighed. A charm for their wedding day, one for each baby, one for ten years, and other things she loved throughout the years. She wore that bracelet every day, even when it was empty.

She turned to her desk to grab a tissue and noticed the voicemail light on their phone was blinking. They rarely got messages, but maybe it was one of the guys calling with a request for the next day's festivities. She picked up the cordless phone from its base and pushed the speed dial button to retrieve it.

"Joey, hey, it's Dan. Look, I just opened your present and it's too much. Really, please let me know how to return it. I'm not sure what you were thinking, but you can't just buy my friendship. And,

I mean, I know it's Christmas and I'm sorry, but...don't contact me again."

CHAPTER SEVENTEEN

THE TRAIN FROM London to Paris takes about two and a half hours. Joey spent approximately one and a half hours trying not to think about Dan, and the rest of the time actively thinking about him. She felt terrible and wanted nothing more than to talk to him, but as the only thing he'd requested was that she not do just that, she decided to respect his request.

She did talk to her parents and Betty on Christmas Day, all three of whom sounded happy, but eager to hang up. She guessed they'd all been together when Dan had opened his present and the initial fallout was even worse than the icy message she received.

How could she have been so stupid? An expensive gift after seven months apart was a terrible idea. Worse, it was cruel. She knew him better than anyone. It didn't matter if someone spent $5 or $500 on a gift for Dan; he was like the poster child for "it's the thought that counts." And even though she'd thought a little about how sending him a nice watch would make her feel, she'd completely ignored how it would seem to him.

As the train pulled into Paris, Joey vowed to leave all thoughts of Dan and the watch fiasco in 2002. They were here to celebrate a new year, and she could be anything she wanted in 2003. Heck, maybe new Joey could actually think of a way to get her life sorted in a way that left everyone around her happy and settled.

Or maybe she could drink enough to stop thinking altogether.

They grabbed a taxi and left the logistics to Taylor. Her French was apparently good enough, because thirty minutes later, they pulled up in front of a gorgeous hotel where men in crisp uniforms appeared immediately to help with the bags. After checking in and sending the luggage to the rooms, Joey suggested a quick stop at the bar to kick off Operation Drunk NYE.

A few glasses of champagne later, Taylor announced that she wanted to take a catnap before getting ready for the evening.

"Brilliant," Joey said. Or maybe she slurred. Either way, she was excited for having such a smart girlfriend.

They made plans to be ready for dinner by seven and stepped into their rooms, where Taylor and Joey both ran to the balcony to check out the view of the Eiffel Tower, kissed because it seemed like the romantic thing to do, then set an alarm and quickly fell asleep in each other's arms.

They awoke bright-eyed and refreshed, as only eighteen-year-old girls can do after a two-hour nap, and popped up to get ready. Joey's other present for Taylor was a shopping trip where they both picked out gorgeous evening gowns for the party, which was listed as black tie. Taylor was better with hair and Joey was better with makeup, so they each helped the other primp until Joey was positive she'd never been so beautiful in her entire life.

As Joey zipped Taylor into her navy-blue Oscar de la Renta, they heard a knock at the door separating their room from the boys.

"My God," Will said as he took in the picture Joey and Taylor made. "Stunning. Both of you."

Liam came in behind him and also gushed, before pretending to be hurt that the girls hadn't commented yet how dapper he and Will looked in their tuxedos.

"It's like we have our very own James Bonds," Joey said. "One for each of us."

"That's better," said Liam. "Just because we can't be all sparkly like you both tonight doesn't mean you don't get to tell us we're beautiful."

The four of them took last looks in the mirror and made their way into the hallway. Liam was talking a mile a minute and Joey shot Taylor a "what's up with him?" look as they got into the elevator. Will seemed to pick up on it, too, and gave him a quick kiss before they entered the lobby.

"Sorry," said Liam. "I guess I'm just a little excited. New Year, new friends, new city, you know."

Joey nodded but had a sneaking feeling something else was up. That suspicion and Liam's jitters quickly abated as they each took a glass of champagne from one of the waiters circling the room. The event began with drinks and appetizers in the ballroom while a band played something jazzy. The whole thing felt very grown up and stood in stark comparison to where Joey had spent this same day the first time around.

Joey and Dan had both picked up jobs at Scottsdale Fashion Square during their first semester at school, and since the holidays are the busiest shopping days of the year, they jumped at the chance for extra hours and overtime pay. They'd both worked until stores closed on Christmas Eve and spent a busy Christmas Day together with their families, leaving little time to catch up on sleep before facing shoppers with arms full of returns the next day.

Joey was exhausted from being on her feet all day, but when a friend who worked with her at Banana Republic mentioned that her dad's company needed a few extra servers for a New Year's Eve party he was throwing, she said yes before thinking it through. And that's how she found herself carrying trays of steaming hors d'oeuvres at a fancy house in the Arcadia neighborhood of Phoenix. She was loading up her tray in the kitchen about an hour before midnight when a frantic, waving hand caught her eye from the back yard.

"Dan!" she nearly yelled in surprise. "Er, damn!" she said, quickly, as the other servers looked over at her. "Stubbed my toe. I'm just gonna catch some fresh air for a sec."

No one was listening to her babble, but she still felt like she should say something before opening the back door and slipping outside. It was cold, but Phoenix-in-December cold, so not too bad. She shivered for a second as she looked around for Dan, but soon felt him wrap her up in one of his trademarked hugs.

"It's almost midnight," he said. "I couldn't let us start a year without a kiss."

"It's not even eleven!" she pointed out, laughing, but turning to face him.

"You didn't let me finish. It's almost midnight...in part of the country. And since I knew you'd be too swamped to get away during Arizona midnight, I thought we'd better have our kiss now. So, I parked down the street and jumped their back fence."

"Well, I don't actually have time now either," she said. "They're going to miss me if I don't hurry back."

"Not a problem," he said. "I'm a super-fast counter. "Tennineeightsevensixfivefourthreetwoone, Happy New Year!"

He kissed her and held her face in his hands, holding her steady as she giggled and tried to catch her breath.

He pulled away, said, "There's more where that came from in 2003," then ran away, presumably to jump the fence again.

When she'd arrived at the apartment later that night, well into the early morning hours, he was asleep on the couch, the video-game controller still in his hand. She laid down on the couch with her head in his lap and felt completely content.

Now, a world away, Joey looked around to see how far she'd come. She wasn't a server at this party; she was a guest. And not at some house back home, but in Paris. Again, she felt like such a grown-up, not at all realizing that only someone who is not a grown-up would call themselves a grown-up.

But yes, very adult things were happening all around her. Taylor could have easily passed for a Parisian woman as she glittered, both figuratively and literally, making polite conversation in French. And now Joey had put on a little weight thanks to their frequent pub visits, she even filled out her evening gown like an actual adult. She was beginning to wish she could do something a little childish to even things out, but it was too late.

A proposal is a very grown-up thing, indeed.

CHAPTER EIGHTEEN

RIGHT THERE, IN the middle of the party, Liam was down on one knee, saying something only Will could hear.

Joey grabbed Taylor's hand as an involuntary "aww!" escaped her lips before she could stop herself. Taylor had gone completely rigid as they watched the scene unfold; it *was* rather shocking.

Will's face went from surprised, to happiness, then suddenly to tears. Liam stood up abruptly, apparently as confused as Joey and Taylor about the shift in reaction. Were they happy or sad tears?

They all got their answer as Will extricated his hand from Liam's and bolted for the door. Liam trailed him closely, but as they were in heels and floor-length dresses, Joey and Taylor fell far behind in their pursuit. By the time they got out of the ballroom and into the lobby, they found a confused and dejected-looking Liam.

"What happened?" asked Taylor.

"I don't know," Liam said. "He seemed excited at first, but then he told me not to follow him and just...left."

"Did you see which way he went?" Joey asked.

Liam pointed to the right and Joey headed for the door, confident that Taylor would take good care of Will. She walked outside and immediately regretted this choice. It was freezing, and not like she was used to back home. She turned on her heel to head back inside, but then saw that Will hadn't gotten very far.

"Yeah, it's too cold for a dramatic exit," he said, seeing her. "You should go back inside."

"I will...if...you will," Joey said, her teeth chattering.

"Oh here." He took his coat off and wrapped her up in it. "It's my fault you're out here. But I can't go back in there."

"There—" Joey pointed across the street. A small souvenir shop was still open, so they made their way to it and pretended to browse while they talked. "Okay, spill," she said, able to talk again now that she didn't feel like a human popsicle.

"I just...panicked," he said. "I mean, we've talked about getting married, but in the future. Not now."

"Have you told him you're not ready?"

"No, and it's not that I'm not ready." Will looked down. "It's everything with my family. I had hoped that bringing Liam home all the time would make it easier, but they seem so happy to think of me with Taylor. That was so foolish of me, but of course they'd prefer that life for their son. It's just so much easier."

Joey wanted to say something comforting, but she found herself at a loss. It was just this kind of conversation she'd hoped to avoid in her own life that had kept her from acknowledging who she really was her whole life. How could she give someone advice on this subject?

Then she remembered something she'd read years ago from one of her favorite writers, who also felt torn between a life that was easy and a life that was her own.

"Will, try something for me," Joey began, hoping she could do Glennon Doyle justice, from memory. "I want you to tell me the most beautiful story you can think of for how your life should be."

Will looked at her and cocked his head but closed his eyes and exhaled. She could tell he was really thinking.

"Take away what everyone else thinks," Joey said, hoping to guide him. "Just tell me what your life looks like."

"It looks how it looks now," Will said, opening his eyes and smiling. "It's me and Liam together, but we don't have to worry about what the rest of the world thinks. We graduate next year and get a place in the city but go home often. And we travel the world together and have a family someday."

"Well, I can't guarantee that you won't have to worry about

the rest of the world. Some people will never accept you, and that is going to hurt. Your own family might not and that is going to more than hurt, if it happens. But if the beautiful story about your life begins and ends with Liam, that's it. The rest will be okay and you can make a life with the people who accept you just as you are."

Will sniffed again as his eyes welled up with tears.

"Happy tears or sad tears?" Joey asked.

"Happy," Will said. "I just got proposed to! On New Year's Eve, in Paris!"

"You sure did." Joey hugged him. "Now maybe you should go finish that proposal by actually giving him an answer?"

They laughed and walked back to the hotel together, and Joey gave him back his jacket before they went back in.

"How do I look?" Will said, straightening his tie and reaching up to smooth his hair.

"Beautiful," Joey said, holding back for a second to let him go in first.

Joey stayed a few steps behind as Will and Liam met each other's gazes and walked toward each other. Behind each of them, Joey and Taylor stood and locked eyes, both trying to convey what had happened while the group was separated, but it didn't take long for them to both see how things ended.

" *Yes*," Will exclaimed, causing other people in the lobby to turn and look. Joey tried to start a round of applause, but as no one had seen the rest of the proposal, only Taylor joined in, before the two of them rushed forward to congratulate their friends.

The rest of the night was a blur of toasts, delicious food, dancing, and many kisses to ring in the new year. They stayed out so late that Taylor joked it was almost midnight back home. As Joey did the time zone math, she realized it was actually almost eleven back home and every part of her that had hoped to forget about Dan that night gave up.

"I can't believe they're engaged," Taylor said as she and Joey got back to their room.

"I know," said Joey. "It's so exciting."

"What did you say to him?" Taylor asked, pulling bobby pins out of her hair.

Joey shared their conversation from the gift shop and felt proud as she told it, but as Taylor scrunched her face more and more, Joey stopped to ask her what was wrong.

"They're just so young. Could you imagine if Dan had proposed to you tonight? I'm so glad you get it. These aren't the years for settling down."

Joey was confused for a moment, but then realized she'd said exactly that in her graduation speech. And she'd meant it, but for her and Dan, not her and Taylor. Sure, she wanted to keep her options open, but if she already knew she was supposed to marry Taylor, would getting engaged soon be so bad?

"Oh, no," Taylor said, watching as Joey thought it through. "I don't mean you said anything wrong to him. That was really beautiful. I'm happy for them. Just also glad it's not us."

As they finally crawled into bed in the early hours of January 1, 2003, Joey wondered what the year would hold for them. She'd been so excited by the question marks as she'd run toward them back in May.

But now, she worried she might not like the answers.

CHAPTER NINETEEN

TAYLOR AND JOEY settled back into school with a renewed sense of excitement. Joey was thrilled for Liam and Will, but Taylor was right; they were so young and there were so many other things to focus on. Joey found herself writing with every spare moment and Taylor picked up extra private lessons to hone her skills.

When they were together, they were as happy as ever. Joey knew they both thrived when they could throw themselves into their art and pretended not to mind how little they saw each other. Or maybe she didn't mind at all?

She certainly didn't mind how productive she was. She'd never known the thrill of typing "the end" at the bottom of a manuscript and cried the first time it happened. Around the fourth or fifth time, she still welled up with tears, but also marveled at the speed with which she could churn them out. She hadn't yet tackled the more personal stories Taylor wanted her to write, but she was waiting to get a few more others under her belt. She wanted to know her own voice before diving into the deeper material.

"It's really good," Taylor said, setting down her latest novel on a cold, windy morning in early February. "They just keep getting better."

Joey smiled and leaned down to give Taylor a kiss. "We should pack," she said, standing back up.

"Are you sure we should go?" Taylor asked.

"They asked us to." Joey shrugged.

She wasn't sure, either, but they'd agreed to go with Will and Liam back to Cornwall to announce the engagement. Since Will's parents were probably expecting him to announce his engagement to Taylor, the whole situation felt terribly awkward. Joey knew, though, that she might have to make a similar visit home one of these days. And since she'd been the one who'd talked Will into saying yes, she felt she owed it to him to be there for moral support in case they needed to make a quick exit.

Taylor began to pack a few basics in the suitcase they shared.

"How did your parents take it?" she said, folding a pair of jeans.

"Uh, I haven't told them."

The silence in the room was louder than any reaction Joey had expected.

"I'm going to, soon," Joey said. "I just thought I should do it in person."

"Oh."

The funny thing about dating a woman, Joey realized, was that she knew exactly what Taylor's "oh" meant. She'd used it on Dan hundreds of times through the years. She knew how she'd want him to react if she said it. She wanted him to be a mind-reader and understand that her "oh" really meant...well, it could mean a lot of things.

The other funny thing about dating a woman, Joey realized, was that even though she actually *could* almost read Taylor's mind in that moment, she was going to pretend she couldn't. She was going to pull a Dan. Or maybe a man. They probably all did this.

Joey kept packing and shifted the subject to her manuscript that Taylor had just finished. She knew Taylor was still upset but appreciated her commitment to pretending like she cared about the manuscript for even a millisecond.

As cowardly as it was, Joey just didn't want to discuss coming out to her parents. She realized she was the world's biggest hypocrite, packing to help a friend come out to his parents when she had no plans to do the same to her own, but couldn't think about that right now. Taylor had done it at such a young age. Of course she was hurt that Joey hadn't yet been brave.

Joey and Taylor finished packing and bundled up for their

walk to the station to meet Will and Liam. As they walked, Joey's pulse quickened as she imagined what Will's parents might say. Would they throw them out immediately? Or maybe just get really quiet and pretend like everything was okay because they were British and that seemed like the more civilized response?

The train ride to Cornwall was normally a fun, lively time for the four of them, but the nervous energy seemed to pull everyone's spirits away from one another and into their own headspace. Joey was normally so good at putting everyone at ease no matter the situation, but she found herself unable to broach any topic other than the one they were walking into.

"Do you want to practice what you're going to say?" she said when they were about halfway there.

Will looked startled but relieved that someone had broken the silence.

"I like that idea," Liam said, reaching for Will's hand. "Shall we give it a go?"

Will nodded but said nothing.

"How about something like 'Mom, Dad, I'm getting married to Liam' and then see where it goes?" offered Taylor.

They all laughed nervously, but Will shook his head.

"Actually, I like that," he said. "Short and sweet."

"And then they'll say, 'how wonderful, son!'" said Joey.

Will laughed, but Liam shifted uncomfortably in his seat.

"No, really," Joey said. "Let's decide what they're going to say and not think about any other options. Because that is the only acceptable response."

She was being delusional, and she knew it, but Will's parents had been so kind and loving on every occasion she'd seen them. They adored Will and even though she knew they would be surprised, she couldn't help but hold out hope for him. And also for her.

"They're probably only going to be disappointed to not get me as a daughter-in-law," Taylor said.

"Now that is true," Will laughed. "They'll be so jealous of Joey's parents."

The tension lifted within the group, but Joey felt it land right between her and Taylor as they both took in what Will said. It implied that they would get married, which Joey knew made Taylor uncomfortable, but it also implied that Joey's parents knew about them, which would make her livid. But it gave Joey a new resolve.

There was no point in telling her parents anything until she and Taylor had a bigger announcement to make. And she had about three months left to decide if that was something either of them actually wanted.

CHAPTER TWENTY

LIAM, JOEY, AND Taylor waited at a nearby café while Will had tea with his parents. They were ready to either arrive with champagne to celebrate or keep the meter running in a taxi to extricate him quickly. When Liam's phone rang, all three of them jumped.

"How did it go?" Liam said. Then he nodded. Then he started to cry.

"Oh no," Joey said, as she and Taylor both reached out to Liam to hug him as he hung up the phone.

"No, no," he said brightly. "He says everything's fine and we should head there now!"

"You're kidding!" said Taylor. "What did they say?"

"He didn't give me details, but he sounds happy, and I don't think he'd invite us there if it had gone badly."

They hugged Liam anyway, but with joyful back pats instead of sad ones, and collected their things. Joey was thrilled and Taylor looked like she might cry too. As Liam walked out, Joey held back a moment and gently grabbed Taylor by the arm.

"When I go home, I'll tell them," she said. "I've put them through so much this year, and they deserve to hear it from me in person."

"I know," Taylor said. "It's such a personal decision and I'm sorry for making you feel badly for not already telling them. I just feel weird that they don't know about me, I guess."

"They do, just not the whole story. They know how close we are and that I'm so happy to be with you. They just don't know *how* happy."

Taylor smiled and they shared a quick kiss before leaving. Joey thought she heard the woman at the table next to them say something about them being indecent, but she was too happy for Will to let that bring her down.

Their stay with Will's family ended up being their best of all time. Will's mom apparently had known he was gay for years and her only surprise was when he'd brought Taylor home.

"She's so wonderful, son," she said to the whole group. "It was cruel of you to let us get so attached. Liam, do you play any instruments?"

They all laughed as Liam went to the piano to play some bad

scales and what he could remember from a year of lessons.

"That's a no, then?" said Will's dad, who had taken the whole thing completely in stride. Apparently, his exact words were, "We do have satellite TV, son. I know how the world works. If you're happy, I'm happy."

"So, if you two are together, does that mean you two are as well?" Will's mom asked, pointing from the boys to the girls.

"We are," Joey said.

"A woman in my gardening club is a lesbian," she said. "Very nice woman. Very sturdy. I'll have to tell her I have two other lesbian friends."

Joey felt the tears on her cheeks before realizing she was crying.

"Oh no, I've said the wrong thing," Will's mom said. "Is that not the right word?"

"No, no." Joey stood to give her a hug. "I think these are happy tears. I'm not sure why I'm crying, actually."

"Joey's actually bisexual," Taylor offered gently. "She was in a long-term relationship with a man before we got together."

"Well now, that's something," Will's dad said. Joey was so impressed. She knew they were throwing a lot of information at him, and he couldn't have been kinder.

"Is it, Dad?" Will looked amused.

"It is. You know, I think I fancied a lad when I was in school, but it wasn't something you could just talk about back then. And then I met your mum and knew she was the one for me. You kids are lucky. You can love who you love and let that be the end of it."

They all let that hang in the air for a bit while Will's mom went to make a few phone calls to share the good news. It wasn't that Joey didn't appreciate what he'd said, but she knew that wasn't true. Maybe things had gotten better since he was younger, and that was certainly encouraging, but even what they were all celebrating was tainted by the fact that Will and Liam's union would not be recognized in a legal sense for years.

Thinking about the future made Joey realize something. Without her, would Will and Liam even be getting married? If she hadn't come back to this timeline, who would be there to talk Will into saying yes? It did seem like his family would be accepting of him, and it wasn't like she'd done anything to convince them, so that should still happen. But he had to say yes to even get to that point.

Looking across the room at Will and Liam cozied up on the couch together, finally able to be a couple in front of family, Joey hoped that, somehow, they'd figured it out in reality. Or was this reality?

"Where'd you go?" Taylor said, bringing her back to the here and now.

Before she could answer, Will's mom came back in with a tray of pastries and a haughty look on her face.

"Well, Cousin Janet didn't take the news well," she said,

putting the tray down. "But no one likes her anyway, so now we have two things to celebrate."

"No Janet at Christmas this year?" said Will's dad.

"Indeed," she said, laughing. "Stupid cow. Good riddance to her and anyone else who can't see what I see."

Will blushed under his mom's loving gaze and it was clear what she was seeing: her son, in love, and finally able to be himself around his parents. It was every parent's dream come true.

Joey let herself do what she tried not to most days and thought about her own kids, waiting for her back in her own timeline. If she chose Taylor, could they still exist? The longer she stayed on this trajectory, the harder it became for her to think of them. But on a day like today, it was impossible not to.

Had any of them ever felt like they couldn't tell her something? She hoped not, but seeing how Will's parents had taken today's news, she wondered why he'd ever thought they'd be anything but supportive. She made a vow to tell them over and over that she'd always love them, no matter what, when she got back to them.

If she got back to them.

CHAPTER TWENTY-ONE

TAYLOR'S MUSIC DEPARTMENT was buzzing in early April when it was announced that a new professor would be finishing the semester with them. A young cellist from France had agreed to work with the school's most promising students, and that definitely included Taylor.

"What if she thinks I'm terrible?" Taylor lamented.

"She won't," said Joey.

"What if she doesn't like me?" Taylor said.

"Impossible." Joey could tell her girlfriend was nervous and decided she should walk her to her first session.

"You don't know that. If she doesn't like me, then she could tell everyone she knows about me and really hurt my chances at finding a job someday."

Joey had never seen Taylor like this and tried to come up with a way to reassure her that everything would work out. Short of saying, "Trust me, you've already worked with her, and everything turns out just fine," she couldn't think of how to help.

"Do you want me to come in with you?" Joey said. "I can talk you up and she'll see how great you are. Or maybe I'll go make a fool of myself near her and you'll look all elegant by comparison."

Taylor laughed and let out a big sigh. Joey didn't know how to charm a fancy, French woman anyway, so the latter option would have made the most sense.

"No, I'm okay." She shook her head and lifted her chin an inch. "I'm just nervous."

They arrived at the music building and Joey pulled Taylor into an empty practice room. She kissed her, then pulled away to smooth her hair for her. "And if that French bitch tries anything, she can answer to me," she said.

"Who is this French bitch you speak of?" came a voice from the corner of the room.

Joey jumped and Taylor let out a mix between a gasp and a little scream as they both turned to see that the room was not, in fact, empty. A woman stood up from behind the piano she'd been seated at and smiled at them.

"I am so sorry," she said. "I did not mean to eavesdrop."

If her accent hadn't given away the fact that she was French, her appearance certainly would have. Joey tried not to let her jaw hang slack as she took in the woman standing before them. She was beautiful and glamorous and unless Joey was mistaken, she was her girlfriend's new professor.

As if she could read Joey's mind, the woman played the first few ominous chords of Beethoven's Fifth Symphony, then laughed.

"I'm Vienne," she said, walking around the piano and toward them with her hand extended. Joey saw Taylor's expression and knew she needed to help ease the tension. It was totally her fault, after all.

"Vienne, I'm Joey," she said, stepping in front of Taylor. "I am so sorry. I didn't mean..."

"Say no more." Vienne shook her hand. "You were being a good friend. And you must be?"

"Taylor," said Taylor. "I'm so excited to work with you, Vienne."

"Taylor," Vienne said warmly, crossing to greet her with a kiss on each cheek. "I've heard so much about you. I'm looking forward to hearing you play. Everyone says you are the best cellist here."

Taylor blushed and Joey couldn't help but wonder if she was reacting to the compliment, or the vixen who'd said it. Okay, no, that was silly. Wasn't it?

"She is," Joey said. "She's absolutely the best cellist in the world."

"See?" Vienne said. "A good friend. And what instrument do

you play, Joey?"

"Oh, I'm here for writing."

"Well, you must send me something of yours to read while I am here," Vienne said. "Now, Taylor, shall we get to work?"

"Right, excuse me." Joey held the door open for them. They'd reserved a different room down the hall and Joey wanted nothing more than to get out of their way. "Nice meeting you, Vienne. And again, sorry."

Vienne smiled and Taylor waved as they turned to make their way down the hallway. Normally, Joey would hang around the building to wait for Taylor, either reading or writing during her rehearsals. Today, though, she couldn't get out of there fast enough.

When Taylor came back to their dorm that evening, Joey wished she'd stuck around.

"You should see her play," she said, on about her fifth minute of gushing about Vienne.

"You said that," Joey said. "See, I told you there was nothing to worry about!"

"Her vibrato is the best I've ever seen," Taylor continued. "She's helping me loosen my wrist, but I don't know if I'll ever be as good as her."

The thought of Vienne touching Taylor gave Joey a pit in her stomach. She couldn't have been the only one who saw what this woman looked like.

"She's, like, really pretty too," Joey said, wanting to gauge

Taylor's response.

"Is she?" Taylor said, turning away.

Well, that settled it. Vienne was obviously gorgeous. If Taylor wasn't acknowledging it, that could only mean one thing: she had a crush on her. Ugh, and Vienne had been so careful to keep referring to Taylor and Joey as just friends. She was probably just as infatuated with Taylor as Joey was. Maybe even more so. Maybe it was a cello thing.

From that day forward, Joey accompanied Taylor to all of her sessions with Vienne and made it a point to kiss Taylor goodbye before every one, right where they were sure to be seen. She couldn't always be there when they finished because she had picked up a new class that overlapped with their rehearsals, but at least she could disabuse Vienne of the notion that she and Taylor were just friends.

Taylor talked less and less about Vienne as time went on, and even complained about her from time to time. She wasn't the French bitch she'd been worried about, but she was hard on her students and expected nothing but the best. As Taylor was already incredible, she pushed her harder than most.

As the semester began to wind down, Joey booked flights for the two of them to fly home for Betty's graduation. Taylor couldn't stay long because she wouldn't be done with her performances until June, but she still wanted to see her family and agreed that she could use a break from playing.

She always seemed flustered right after her time with Vienne, so Joey decided to skip class one afternoon. She stopped by a flower shop after walking Taylor to rehearsal, grabbed her favorite kind of chocolate from a shop on campus, and waited outside the room for her to come out.

She heard the music in the room stop and hopped up from where she'd been sitting on the ground in the hallway to look in through the window in the door. She thought it would be funny if Taylor looked over to see her making a silly face and holding the flowers. Before she could cross her eyes, though, she saw Vienne take Taylor's hand in hers. Taylor's back was to the door, so she couldn't see her expression.

But she could see Taylor tilt her head and lean closer to Vienne. At that same moment, Vienne saw Joey and said something she couldn't hear, but whatever it was made Taylor turn around and bolt to the door she was now standing stupidly in front of.

"Joey!" Taylor said, following her down the hallway. "Nothing happened."

Joey stopped and faced her.

"But would something have happened if I hadn't been there?"

Taylor's hesitation was all she needed to hear. She dropped the flowers and the chocolate, turned, and ran.

CHAPTER TWENTY-TWO

"NOTHING HAPPENED," TAYLOR said again when they were back in their dorm.

"But you wanted it to," Joey said. "I saw the look in your eyes."

"You're suffocating me. Why were you even in that building to begin with? I feel like you never let me out of your sight."

Joey couldn't believe Taylor was turning this around on her. Sure, she liked to walk Taylor to her rehearsals, but wasn't that just being a good girlfriend?

"I haven't made any friends this year because we're always together," Taylor said. "Vienne is one of the only people I talk to, other than you, Will, and Liam. I just got confused. And to be honest, I've only ever kissed you. Maybe I thought for a second that I'd just see what it was like."

Joey felt her two selves battling inside her head. The version of her who had lived an extra twenty years knew that Taylor was right about the suffocating thing. Joey had a one-track mind, and it was all Taylor. That kind of love is intense and unhealthy. But the nineteen-year-old side of her felt like it was the only way to be with someone. Why couldn't Taylor see that she just loved her so much?

"Maybe you should kiss her," Joey said quietly.

"Come on," Taylor said.

"No, I mean it. If I wasn't here this year, you'd have dated other girls. You'd have all these friends and have gotten to experience so much more. I care about you and don't want you wondering if there's something better out there. The whole 'if you love someone, let them go' adage is true. Maybe you should go on a date with Vienne and see how you feel."

Taylor was quiet and clearly trying to read Joey's face for any sign that she was kidding.

But Joey wasn't kidding. She knew what her life was like with someone else and had plenty of time to think it through. Maybe things with Taylor weren't perfect, but if their first year together was hard, maybe that was a good thing. It certainly felt better than thinking you were with someone who would love you forever only to find out in twenty years that it wasn't true.

Taylor couldn't have that same certainty if she never even

seriously considered someone else. If Joey wanted them to be together forever, she had to be brave enough to send her out with the world's hottest French cellist.

"You're serious," Taylor said. "You want me to go on a date with Vienne?"

"I do." Joey nodded. "I can stay at a hotel and write for a few days, and you can pretend I'm not here. You're right about me smothering you. I am so sorry, Taylor."

"I don't know what to say. Are you going to date someone else while you're away?"

"No, no. I know my heart. I know it's yours. But I don't want you to resent me for keeping you to myself. I'll stay away for a week, but then I'll also give you more space if and when you want me to come back."

Taylor crossed the room and kissed Joey harder than she had in a while, and Joey's body sagged in relief as she answered the kiss and put her arms around her girlfriend. How had she let things get so intense while trying to get away from a love that had overwhelmed her at the same age?

Joey knew better than anyone about the kind of resentment she had been fostering in Taylor. Hadn't she always wondered if Dan was the right one for her because she'd never dated anyone else? The thoughts were fleeting because they really were so happy together, but they'd come and gone through the years and were especially intense leading up to the reunion.

The best thing she could do for Taylor, and herself, really, was to give them some space. A week might not be enough, but it was a good place to start. And she really did want to write. She had plenty to say in the novel she'd been outlining for months now, and it was time to get it all out before her final projects were due.

As she started to pack, Taylor looked at her quizzically.

"You're leaving right now?" she said.

"Well, I thought I'd better go before I change my mind. Do you want me to stay?"

"One more night." Taylor took the clothes she had pulled from the closet out of her hands. "You just gave me the greatest gift and I want to say thank you."

Taylor kissed her again and pulled her down to the bed. They were so used to each other now that their routine had become predictable, but Joey felt a difference in Taylor that made every touch feel electric.

She thrives when she feels understood. Joey knew this feeling well. She'd felt herself react similarly on days when Dan had gone out of his way to make her feel special. Whether it was getting up at midnight to feed a crying baby or stopping for takeout on the way home from work on a day when she was too exhausted to cook, she knew how much it meant to be taken care of.

Joey wondered how she could keep this feeling with Taylor alive, long term. Being together every free moment of the day was clearly not the answer. Taylor had already figured out exactly how

Joey wanted to be loved and she'd given her just what she needed. It was her turn to do the same.

They spent the night wrapped up in each other's arms and Joey tried not to think about Taylor in a similar situation with Vienne, but she couldn't help herself. It was hypocritical and she knew it, especially with how understanding Taylor had been of Joey's admission that she still loved Dan. But that was before. Or was it? Even though they hadn't spoken in months, Joey had to admit that Dan was always on her mind. She might not say it, but Taylor knew her well enough to know she hadn't just forgotten him.

Suddenly, an idea popped into her head that made the whole world right again. If Taylor wanted her back after their week apart, that was the last sign she needed. In addition to writing while she was away, Joey would do a little shopping.

It was time to pick out a ring.

CHAPTER TWENTY-THREE

JOEY CHECKED HERSELF into a hotel the next day and told Taylor to call if she wanted more time, but otherwise she'd be back in a week. She picked a hotel near Hyde Park so she could walk through it when the weather was clear and was happily surprised that it was sunny just after she dropped off her bags.

It was good to be outside because she started to panic. Had she really just sent the woman she loved into the arms of someone else? Was it too late to call the whole thing off?

As she walked along the winding path, she felt restless. Moving felt good, but it wasn't quite enough. It was time to write.

She headed back to her hotel room and looked at her notes. She'd been purposely leaving the end of her story open, but decided it was time to use her novel as the ultimate pro/con list. She would write everything she'd outlined so far, but finish this time with her main character going back to the man she loves. She'd write a happy ending for the woman left behind, then see how it all felt to see the ending written out like that.

Then, in a new draft, she'd choose door number two. Maybe whichever version was easier to write was the right answer. She was giving Taylor a week to think things through and take stock of everything; she should do the same.

She knew she could still see herself with Taylor, but if things ended badly, she could fly home and beg Dan to forgive her. They'd already bought tickets to be there for Betty's graduation. One way or another, that trip would seal her fate.

She sat down to write and was amazed at how easily the words came. Her outline had kept the story churning in her brain for so long and it was such a relief to finally get the words out of her. She wrote for as long as she could each day, taking short breaks to eat and do a lap around the park so she wouldn't get too stiff. On one of her walks, she decided to go a little further and stumbled past an antique shop. The window display was lovely, and she decided to take a peek inside.

The woman running the shop was old and kind, but a bit too chatty. Joey was about to leave when she noticed a case of jewelry by the door and couldn't help but look inside. She'd been planning to stop by a shop specializing in engagement rings, but an Art Deco ring in the back of the case caught her eye.

"Lovely, aren't they?" the shopkeeper said, coming up behind her.

"That one," she said, pointing to the ring. "May I see it?"

"Of course, dear. We can't just wait around for a man to buy us something special."

Joey decided to spare this woman the story of what she had planned for the ring and put it on her own hand to admire it. It really was beautiful. Even if she didn't end up giving it to Taylor, she knew it would haunt her forever to leave it at the shop.

A realization struck her. "My purse. I left it at the hotel."

"It'll keep," the woman said. "I'll put it away till the end of the day if you like, dear."

Joey thanked her and walked briskly back to the hotel. She was walking so determinedly she didn't even notice Taylor in the lobby until she did a double take.

"What are you doing here?" she said, slowing her pace and changing direction.

"I came to see you," Taylor said. She was dressed in the new spring coat Joey had bought her and looked radiant. Joey worried that the time apart had given her that glow. Or worse, that her date with Vienne had.

Joey guided her to her room, not sure if she should be thankful or angry with herself for telling Taylor where she was staying. It had seemed prudent, but Joey didn't want to cause a scene in this fancy

London hotel and she didn't know how she'd take the news that her girlfriend was leaving her for someone else.

She chastised herself for thinking so negatively as they walked from the elevator to her room and thought about the ring she'd left behind. If Taylor was here with good news, that was most definitely a sign that she should hurry back to buy it.

"How was your date?" Joey asked, once they were safely in her room. She wasn't sure she wanted to know the answer to that question but best to get right to it.

"It was lovely," Taylor said.

Joey winced but tried to will her face to not show how much those words hurt.

"Vienne is kind, and beautiful, and straight," Taylor said, with a nervous laugh.

"She's straight?"

"Oh, yes. She was happy to have dinner with me but made sure to drop her boyfriend's name into the conversation about twenty times before the salad came."

"But I thought..."

"Yes, I did too. I'm not sure what she would have done if I'd kissed her that day, but I don't think it would have been her kissing me back."

"So, nothing happened this week?" Joey asked.

"Not nothing. I realized how much I love you."

"That's definitely not nothing."

"And I got to know a few of the other girls in my classes. I've got a few new friends."

"That all sounds delightful. But don't you want more time? I'm relieved you didn't do anything with Vienne, but I don't want you to resent me."

"Joey, you've shown me you can give me the freedom I need, and that's all that matters. I was worried we were moving too fast, but if you can be this generous, I could never resent you."

Taylor moved closer to kiss her, but Joey took a step back.

"Could you give me just a minute? I actually came back here to grab my purse," she said. "There's just a quick errand I need to run and then I'll be right back."

"Uh, okay," Taylor said, clearly confused.

"It'll all make sense in about fifteen minutes." Joey guided Taylor to sit on the love seat by the window. "You just wait right here. You look so beautiful, by the way."

Taylor blushed and Joey kissed her on the forehead. She really did look beautiful. And she'd been the one to end their time apart. The signs couldn't be any clearer. On the way to the elevator, Joey checked her reflection in the mirror. She was a little flushed from her walk, but otherwise she looked good. She knew Taylor didn't care how she looked, but she thought it was important to look nice when proposing to someone.

The shopkeeper was thrilled to see her back so soon and had found a nice box to put the ring in.

"In case you don't want to wear it just yet," she said, closing the lid and handing it to her.

Joey tried to walk slowly back to the hotel but felt herself nearly skipping on the way back. She could see everything so clearly now and couldn't wait for the rest of her life to begin.

"Honey, I'm home," she said in a singsong voice as she opened the door to the room.

Taylor wasn't sitting where Joey had left her. In fact, she wasn't sitting at all. She was standing at the window, holding a stack of papers and staring down at them.

"What the hell is this?" was all she said.

CHAPTER TWENTY-FOUR

"DID YOU HEAR me?" Taylor's voice brought Joey back to reality. "I said what the hell is this?"

The ring in Joey's pocket suddenly felt like it weighed twenty pounds. Whatever was about to happen, it was certainly not a proposal.

"That's my outline," Joey said. "For the book I'm writing."

"Yes, I managed to put that together," Taylor said, flipping through the pages. "But what's all this about the main character leaving her girlfriend to go back to the love of her life?"

"It's fiction." Joey knew how flimsy the defense was even as she said it.

"It doesn't seem that way to me." Taylor threw the papers

across the room. "It feels like you writing about using me as an experiment to see if you're actually bisexual before going off to start your life with Dan."

"But that's just one of her options," Joey said. "Did you keep reading?"

"Oh, you mean the part where the girlfriend meets someone else, so it's all okay?"

She'd forgotten about that part. Ouch, how could she have written that down? Especially now, when the thought of Taylor with someone else felt like just about the worst thing that could happen?

"Yes, I wrote that. But that was before—"

"Before you realized Dan doesn't love you anymore?" Tears streamed down Taylor's face. "I can't believe I've spent this whole year thinking we had moved past all that, only to find you think of me as nothing more than a placeholder."

"You're not a placeholder. And this has nothing to do with Dan. Look—" She fumbled in her pocket and pulled out the ring. "I was actually planning to propose before we go home."

Taylor looked at the ring, then back at Joey, her eyes softening slightly after a couple of stares at each.

"We're nineteen," was all she said.

"Well, yeah, but..." Joey began.

"Joey, we're nineteen years old. Why on earth would you propose to me?"

Joey closed the ring box and set it down on the desk, playing for time. How was Taylor simultaneously mad at her for possibly still having feelings for Dan, but also pissed that she wanted to marry her?

"Because I love you and I want to be with you?"

Taylor raised her eyebrows, putting one hand on her hip.

"Because I love you and I want to be with you," Joey said again, this time taking the question out of it. "I've had a lot of time to think about this and it doesn't matter what I wrote on that paper. I choose you."

"Joey," Taylor said, relaxing her posture. "I'm not a choice you get to make right now."

She sat down on the bed and gestured for Joey to join her. Instead, Joey pulled the chair out from her desk and faced her. It felt like a face-to-face moment.

"I think you put too much pressure on us, right from the start," Taylor began. "I know you love me, but I've wondered since the minute you ran away from graduation if maybe you don't just love the idea of me. I'm not all women, I'm just me."

"I don't think of you as all women," Joey said.

"Your notes make me think otherwise. The choice doesn't feel like you're choosing between Dan and me. It feels like you're choosing between being with a man or a woman." Before Joey could let this sink in, Taylor continued, "And like I said, I'm not here for you to choose."

"But I thought you love me?" Joey said.

"I do. Of course I do. But we're nineteen. And living away from home for the first time. We've gotten to have this beautiful year together, but I'm not ready to settle down. I want to be able to take a job with a symphony that travels the world and not have to worry about what it means for us. I want you to write and lock yourself away for months at a time if that's what you need, without a care in the world. I want to be with you if it makes sense for us both, but we're so young."

Joey nodded and cringed with shame. She was older, technically, and should have known all of this. Had she really let Dan's request to cut off communication send her into such a tizzy she had thought her only option was to try to win him back, or lock Taylor down for life?

She knew better than most what could happen to someone who got married before they were ready. Sure, it could lead to eighteen happy years of marriage, but that nineteenth one was a disaster.

Wait. Eighteen happy years. One bad year. She let her brain do the math and gasped. Ninety-five percent of her marriage with Dan had been wonderful. Practically perfect. How had she been willing to give all that up for the 5 percent that hurt?

It wasn't that simple, of course. Before she'd left for the reunion, Dan said they needed to talk. She was pretty sure he was going to ask for a divorce, but what if she didn't let him? What if she fought for him, and for their kids, and they did what Joey and Dan always did best: solved the problem as a team?

She was still mad that he hadn't told her about London, but he was eighteen, and probably scared of losing the love of his life.

Scared that she'd do exactly what she'd done to him in this timeline.

Flying back to Arizona to beg for his forgiveness no longer seemed like the right answer.

It was time to go back and meet her Fate.

CHAPTER TWENTY-FIVE

ULTIMATELY, IT WAS Taylor who suggested that Joey fly back home for Betty's graduation alone. It would give them both time to think and with so many big conversations taking place, Joey was thankful for the space. She was also thankful to not have to explain her relationship with Taylor. As far as anyone back home knew, they were just friends, and even though that classification made Joey's stomach clench, she didn't want to take any extra attention away from Betty's big day than her return already would.

Arriving back at Heathrow alone nearly a year to the date she'd arrived felt even more surreal than landing there with Taylor had the year before. Everything looked exactly the same, but she couldn't help but notice the subtle differences in her reflection as she approached the automatic door to her terminal.

She looked older, but not how she remembered looking at nineteen in the before. Back then, she was a bride-to-be, excitedly working out and eating right so she'd look perfect on her wedding day, even though she was already in the best shape of her life. Now, she had softer edges, wider hips, an actual chest she no longer had to pad a bra to see, and the furrowed brow of a young woman facing big decisions and tough conversations.

She wondered what Dan would think of the new her. She wondered how he would seem to her, with both fresh eyes and new experiences under her belt. She ached for him but tried not to get her hopes up. She'd been so sure about Taylor only a week ago and knew she owed it to all of them to not rush things, not this time.

As she handed her passport to the attendant at the check-in counter, the name on her badge brought Joey back to the present. Mary. Joey smiled and made polite conversation ("yes, back home for a visit, here for school," etc.), but then sighed as she walked away. In her carry-on, she had the scrap of paper with an address for Mary Fate and the secret hope that everything that had happened could be undone if her homecoming didn't go as planned.

But what was the actual plan? She knew she needed to talk to Dan, but there were two problems. One. He had never gone back on the "don't contact me" request. Two. It was so much more than just one conversation. Maybe he'd be willing to go away with her for a weekend? Their anniversary was coming up and they always liked to get away to Sedona for at least a night to celebrate.

What am I thinking? An anniversary that never happened couldn't be celebrated. And asking Dan to go away with her when she didn't even know if he'd acknowledge her suddenly felt like an absurd request. She'd have to start small. Maybe just a little chat at the graduation, with plenty of people around. She hadn't even confirmed he'd be at the graduation, but hopefully he could put his anger for her away for Betty's sake.

As she walked by the bank of monitors with the departure and arrivals, she double-checked her gate information and that the flight was on time. It was and she once again did the mental math to check that she'd arrive in time for the ceremony. Booking her flight to land on the actual date of Betty's graduation was risky, but there weren't daily flights to Phoenix and she was already cutting it close with her school finals schedule. Luckily, her professors had allowed her to turn in her end-of-year projects early. The little details lining up felt like a good omen.

And as she got herself situated in her seat for the long flight, Joey let the emotional exhaustion she'd been feeling for weeks now finally catch up to her. She fell asleep, hoping she was right about good things to come.

As she landed in Phoenix, the evening desert sunshine made her eyes hurt as she looked out of the window. She was on the left side of the plane and could see Arizona State University and wondered if Dan was there right now, about to drive west, like she was.

She pulled her cell phone from her purse once they had arrived at the gate and turned it on, excited to see service bars for the first time in a year. This was a bold idea, but maybe just what she needed to break the ice.

She held down the number 1 on the keypad and it dialed Dan's number. No answer.

"Hey, it's, uh, Joey. I just landed and thought maybe we could ride to the school together. Sorry, this is silly. Not even sure you'll be there. Never mi—"

Her voice cut off when the phone started to ring.

"Hello?" she said hopefully, gathering her belongings as the rows in front of her deplaned.

"Hey," said Dan. His voice was both familiar and foreign. Had he changed this year just as much as she had?

"Oh, hey. I was just leaving you a message. I saw ASU from the plane and wondered...well, I'm at the airport."

"You're calling for a ride?" he asked. She couldn't tell what the emotion was in his voice, but decided that since he hadn't hung up, she'd keep going.

"Yeah, I mean, I don't need one, I can get a taxi. I just thought maybe we could talk."

There was a long pause as he pondered this. Or maybe he was pondering what names to call her.

"Yeah, I can pick you up."

"Really? I thought you weren't talking to me." She held the

phone with her shoulder as she made her way down the aisle.

"Where do you want me to pick you up?" Okay, he was ignoring that. Probably for the best.

"Terminal Four, south side, uh, door two?"

"I'll be there in fifteen," he said, before hanging up.

It had to have been the coldest phone exchange of their lives. He was talking to her, which was a good start, and was clearly planning to go to the graduation. More good omens. But the tone of his voice alerted Joey immediately that she was not going to be picked up by the nineteen-year-old Dan she once knew. If anything, he sounded more like the Dan she'd left behind in 2022. Had their year apart accelerated that transformation?

She'd been hoping for a reset to avoid that fate and now felt terrified she'd somehow brought it about twenty years too early. He wasn't supposed to hate her yet. He wasn't supposed to hate her ever, preferably, but this just felt wrong. And now she was going to be stuck in rush hour traffic heading to an outdoor event in heat she hadn't been around in a year.

It was going to be an uncomfortable night.

CHAPTER TWENTY-SIX

DAN DIDN'T LOOK all that different at first glance, but his car most certainly did. As she stepped out to the curb at Sky Harbor and felt the blow-dryer-like wind hit her face, she squinted and looked for the 1995 Toyota Camry she and Dan used to share. It wasn't until she heard her name three times that she finally realized the man sitting in the car directly in front of her was talking to her.

"You coming?" Dan opened his door and stood to add a wave to the name-calling.

"Whose car is this?" she said, walking toward him, confused.

"Whose boobs are those?" he said, meeting her at the back of the car to help load her bags in the trunk.

They laughed and stood awkwardly behind the car until the

person behind them honked. They didn't hug, but both were processing a lot of new things. As Joey slid into the passenger seat, she realized this car was very new, and very unlike Dan.

"Yes, yes, the car is new," he said, making his way through the throngs of vehicles to get them to the freeway. "I got a job this year and saved up."

"At the mall?" She wondered how on Earth he'd been able to save so much while making minimum wage, and without her to help with the rent.

"No, at my dad's office."

"But that's up by our house."

"Yeah, so it was pretty convenient. We carpool."

"But what about the apartment?"

"What apartment?" Dan asked, trying to keep the car straight while shooting her a look.

Right. She wasn't supposed to know about the apartment. And because she hadn't been here to live with him, he'd probably broken the lease. And stayed home. And since she wasn't here to occupy his time, he'd started at an office job years earlier than he had in their timeline.

"Oh, I thought Betty said something about you moving out. Sorry. But why did you start a job so early? You said we had plenty of time to be shut up in an office when we're older."

"Well, when I suddenly had nothing to do last summer, Dad asked if I wanted to work with him full-time until school started.

Then I realized how much money I could save by staying home and making good money, so I adjusted my schedule to only be on campus Tuesdays and Thursdays. I work long days Monday, Wednesday, and Friday, but I've got some downtime to do homework, so it works out pretty well."

Joey felt those first words sting, but she was so thankful the car had given them something to talk about. And since Dan was driving, she could look at him without feeling awkward. She wanted to take in the full picture.

He looked older at nineteen than he had before, just like she did. She wasn't sure what she was expecting. A broken-hearted kid whom she'd have to put back together? Okay, maybe that was kinda what she thought, but that most definitely wasn't what she was seeing. In this new car and nice clothes, he looked closer to how he had at thirty when they were finally able to catch up on some bills and the kids were all old enough to sleep through the night.

Her absence really had accelerated his timeline, it seemed. He wasn't broken at all. He looked good. Really good, if she was being honest.

"I drank a lot of beer," Joey said abruptly. "Well, cider actually."

"Uh, okay?" Dan said with a laugh.

"You asked about my boobs." She realized she was answering a question they'd since moved past.

"Ah, right. Sorry, I just almost didn't recognize you. It's not just that. You look older."

"So do you. I mean that in a good way."

"Yeah, I did too."

They sat in uncomfortable silence, letting the events from a year ago fill up every available inch around them. The anger, the confusion, the hurt; it all hung in the air, just waiting for one of them to address it.

"I'm sorry," Joey said at last.

"It's fine," Dan said. "Ancient history."

"It's not fine."

"I mean I'm fine. And this is probably a better conversation for another time. I don't want to show up for Betty feeling all emotional about things that happened a long time ago."

"A long time ago? It's been a year."

"Yes, a year. And a lot can happen in a year."

He said it with an edge to his voice and Joey desperately wanted to ask more. Was a year enough time for him to fall completely out of love with her? Enough time to realize that all he ever wanted was her, still?

For the moment, they seemed to at least be cordial. It was a huge weight off her shoulders just to be near him again without him yelling at her for everything she'd done. She deserved it. Or did she?

"Can I ask you something?" she said.

"You can," he said. "But I don't promise to answer."

"Fair enough." She drew in her breath and continued, "Why did you keep my letter? The one telling me I got a scholarship to the school in London?"

"Why did I what?" Once again he looked so distracted she immediately regretted asking him this on a busy Phoenix freeway.

"My letter. Taylor said you brought it to her, thinking it was for her, but then you never showed it to me." In all the times she'd thought about asking him this question, she realized she'd assumed it would be through tears. But just as he seemed to have found some peace and patience in their year apart, she realized she had too.

"Is that what you think?" Dan said as a single tear fell to his cheek.

"What am I supposed to think, Dan?" Joey was surprised at his reaction. "You had our whole future planned out and didn't want to risk what would happen if I went to London, so you kept that letter from me."

Dan's hands gripped the steering wheel so hard his knuckles turned white. He brushed the tear away, and when he replied, his voice was cold.

"Joey, I didn't keep that letter," he said matter-of-factly. "And I don't know what little story you've been telling yourself about that, but if this is why you ran away, I..."

"You what?"

Dan shook his head. "Look, this is a big night for Betty. For all of us, actually. I'm glad you're here and really don't want to get into everything. I probably shouldn't have picked you up, but I thought...I guess I thought we could clear the air and that would be a good thing before everything else."

Everything else? A big night for everyone? Joey wanted to ask more questions about all of that but had to know right now what he meant about the letter.

"Tell me," she said. "The letter? I know you had it."

"I did," he said. "And since you never mentioned it, I figured you got it, but decided to just stick with our plan. Until you ran away, that is."

"But you never gave it to me."

"You weren't home when I stopped by with it. So I gave it to Betty."

Chapter Twenty-Seven

IT MUST HAVE been a hundred degrees outside, but Joey suddenly felt like she was back in London on a January night.

Betty. Her little sister had kept the letter from her, knowing how much she'd dreamed of going to school for writing. Why would she have done that?

"Stop," Dan said.

"What?"

"Stop whatever you're thinking. Maybe she set it down somewhere and it ended up in a junk mail pile or something. You cannot confront her about this. Not tonight."

"I really don't think you get to tell me what I can and can't do," Joey said haughtily.

"After everything you put me through, I think I absolutely can." Dan's tone was icy.

That was a decent point, but this was about her and Betty, so she thought for a minute about ignoring him. Tonight really didn't seem like the best time for a full-on sister screaming match. And as she had been the one who had abruptly ran away from her own high school graduation, she did probably owe her parents an uneventful one for her little sister.

But inside, she was fuming. Somehow, she knew the letter hadn't been set aside. She didn't know why Betty would have kept it from her, but kept it from her she had, and that one decision had kicked off a series of events that had altered her life forever. For better? Sitting next to bizarro Dan made her feel like that was a definite no.

The Dan she knew at this age was broke, but full of joy. Now, here he was, driving a fancy car, maybe even the owner of an actual savings account, and utterly devoid of the happiness and humor she'd come to love in him. And who was she kidding? She had money in the bank, a computer full of completed novels, and she probably looked equally as sad as he did. Maybe she was just projecting.

"Are you happy?" she asked.

"Right now, or in general?" he said, giving her a sideways glance.

"Both, I guess."

He paused to think. "Yes," he said. "A year ago, I didn't think I ever would be again, but I really am. And I'm sorry for getting into all of this today, but I really am happy. It's a big day and I'm glad you're here for it."

Well, that was good news, at least. And leave it to Dan to go full-on big brother for Betty's graduation. She'd always been a little third-wheely with them and as her sister, Joey was always more annoyed than understanding. But Dan loved Betty and always did a great job of making her feel included whenever he could.

One of the few fights they'd had as teenagers had been about that same issue, now she thought about it. Betty had asked Dan to find her a date to his senior prom so she could go with them. Dan had been willing and knew it wouldn't be hard to find a guy at his school who would jump at the chance for a date with Betty, but Joey wanted the night to be just theirs. She couldn't keep Betty from going to her own senior prom at Conquistador because she was a junior there and had her pick of guys in the senior class.

But Dan's prom was the night Joey had been hoping could be their first time. She eventually changed her mind, but during the weeks leading up to it, she spread the rumor among Dan's friends that Betty wasn't available that night. Several of them looked pretty bummed and she felt badly about it eventually, but it ended up being one of the few big events in hers and Dan's relationship that Betty didn't get to be at, and she was secretly thankful.

Everyone knew Dan would be crowned prom king and when

Betty said she wanted to be there to see that moment, she'd rolled her eyes, while Dan had promised to see what he could do. Alone on the driveway that night, Betty had been petulant, and Dan was annoyed, still oblivious to Joey's plans of a rose petal covered bed at a hotel. She really thought she was doing him a favor by keeping Betty away, but it wasn't one of her better moments.

It made sense that Dan would be defending her now. Had they talked about Joey a lot after she'd disappeared? Of course they would have, at first, she assumed. No one else in the world would understand what they were going through, other than each other. And when Joey had called home after a while, Betty had specifically asked if she'd forgive her, one free pass.

The letter. Joey realized in an instant that Betty had been covering her tracks for the letter. Now Joey had gone to the school anyway, Betty must have been ready to confess. Or must have thought it would come up eventually. Maybe the school would ask about it and she'd have to come clean. So it wasn't a premeditated question after all.

Joey knew she had hurt a lot of people and complicated multiple lives with her decision last year. If Betty was willing to forgive her, she could do the same. This realization couldn't have come at a better time, as she noticed Dan was exiting the I-17 on Dunlap, and they were almost to the school.

"I won't bring up the letter," Joey said. "Not tonight, not ever."

"Thank you," Dan said with a sigh. "I really don't know what happened, but you got there anyway, so no harm no foul, right?"

"I wouldn't say no harm. And I really am sorry and want to talk to you another time about all of this, but I won't blame that letter for my decisions. It might have been the catalyst, but the decisions were mine."

Dan winced but nodded. Maybe it had been easier for him to think there was something to blame for her abandoning him, but he'd found his way back to happiness, and she couldn't wait to hear all the details. Heck, he'd agreed to drive her here today, and that was already so much more than she'd hoped for.

As they parked, Joey looked again at Dan, trying not to project everything she was feeling. Yes, he was different, but so was she. Maybe there was a way for her to fit into this new Dan's life. And maybe whatever was going to cause their issues in nineteen years had already come to pass, meaning their marriage could be 100 percent happy, or as close to it as possible. If she had run away in the first place because she thought he'd kept a letter from her and that wasn't the case, what was keeping them apart now?

She vowed to keep these thoughts to herself until tomorrow and walked toward the football field next to Dan, glad the uncomfortable night she'd envisioned seemed to be very different than the one she was experiencing.

After all, how much could happen at a high school graduation?

CHAPTER TWENTY-EIGHT

"JOEY GIRL!"

Joey heard her mother's voice from somewhere up in the bleachers and scanned the crowd for her face. Before she could find her, though, she felt a crushing hug and realized Dad had found her first.

"Daddy!" she yelled, turning around to try to match the hug with her own, less-strong arms. As she squeezed, she felt her mom join them and tried not to cry as she let them both hold her for the first time since about an hour before her own graduation. She failed and was a blubbering mess when they finally pulled apart.

Dan was no longer by her side but must have gone up to help save the seats her mom had been in. Probably better that way, as her parents were now talking over each other with questions and exclamations.

"How was your flight? Have you gotten taller? I hardly recognized you! Our little world traveler! You're so grown up! Did you take a cab? I told you I'd come pick you up."

And then together, bringing her back in for a hug, "I missed you so much."

"I missed you both too," she said.

"We should sit," Dad said. "This thing is about to start. Promise you'll stick around to the end of this one?"

He laughed at his own joke as they climbed the steps to the row where a stressed-out Dan sat, trying to save enough room for them all to sit together.

"I'll go find a different spot," he said sheepishly, realizing there was no way they'd all fit.

"Don't be silly," Mom said. "We can ask people to scooch."

"No, it's fine." Dan still looked a little frazzled. "I've got a couple friends down in the front and I can join them."

Joey tilted her head at the looks her parents exchanged over her head as she sat down.

"What?" she said. "We're fine. He gave me a ride here."

"He did?" her dad asked.

"Yes, and we talked about everything." Noticing their shocked expressions, she quickly added, "Not everything, but we'll talk more tomorrow. Or soon."

"Oh," her mom said, looking uncomfortable.

Joey knew she'd put them all through so much and felt awful that she had brought all of this back into their lives on what should have been an exciting night.

"Hey, we're okay," she said. "Really. I'm here for Betty and that's all that matters."

Again, her parents exchanged a look she couldn't decipher, but the graduates were beginning to walk onto the field and she decided to chalk it up to the fallout of her sudden disappearance and reappearance.

Joey strained her eyes trying to pick out Betty in a sea of black caps and gowns. Then she laughed when she realized it wouldn't be hard at all. While a few of the graduates had put cute designs on the tops of their caps, only one had decorated theirs with pink and silver tinsel so she looked like Punk Rock Barbie Graduation Doll. Joey remembered with a laugh that she'd joked about doing the same thing the first time she'd watched her graduate. Something must have happened this year to make her bolder.

Joey smiled, wondering what other changes the year had brought for her little sister. The whole event proceeded just as Joey remembered it would, including the typical graduation speeches, which this time reminded her of her own. She looked for Dan, seated about twenty rows in front of her, and tried to read his mind by looking at the back of his head.

She used to be able to do it, but she wondered if new Dan's

brain worked the same. She tried to hear him and found herself only able to hear what she thought he might be thinking. How this time last year, the love of his life had given one of those speeches and essentially publicly dumped him. How he'd looked for her on the field, a ring heavy in his pocket, realizing she'd run away. Then later realizing just how far she'd run away.

But those thoughts should have made his shoulders sag. She only had his body language to work from and his posture definitely did not seem to be that of a man who was dejected and agonizing over lost love. He sat up straight, occasionally talking or listening to the friends on either side of him. Maybe he was trying to distract himself. All Joey could think about in those stands was what she had done last year, and she knew she wasn't alone.

Her parents were still being weird, and she could tell by the way people quickly looked away that others in the stands knew what she had done. It wasn't every year the valedictorian took off running after the ceremony.

She tried to shake these thoughts and to focus her attention back to Betty. She was definitely going to forgive her for the letter thing, but that didn't mean she couldn't ask about it at some point. She had to.

Joey looked down at Dan and absentmindedly tried to read his mind again, but all she could do was try to see where he was looking. He was staring toward the graduates, which made sense, and it looked like he was looking at or near Betty. She was impossible to ignore, but he seemed to be singularly focused. He was much closer to the field than she was and would probably get to her before Joey and her parents did.

Maybe he didn't want Joey to confront Betty about the letter because he wanted to first? If Joey had torpedoed their whole lives because she thought Dan had betrayed her, it would make sense that he wanted to talk with her about it. In typical big brother fashion, he wanted to protect her from a fight with Joey, but that didn't mean he didn't want answers.

Joey relaxed as everything seemed to make more sense. Her parents were tense because she and Dan had arrived together. Dan was happy but needed answers just like she did. Betty was...Betty. All sparkly and blissfully unaware of the chain reaction she had caused with one decision.

As the graduates threw their caps in the air, Joey watched as Dan joined the crowd of people who were trying to reach their loved ones on the field. She and her parents held back to let the rows in front of them leave, and Joey sighed and hoped Dan would either ask gently or hold off for another day. She loved how he always wanted to have the hard conversations to protect her from them.

Joey smiled as she saw him reach Betty, scooping her up in a hug and twirling her around the way he used to do with her.

She froze as she saw him kiss her longer than a brother would normally kiss a sister.

And as Dan dropped to one knee in front of Betty, Joey let out a blood-curdling scream.

CHAPTER TWENTY-NINE

THE SCREAM WAS just inside her head, but her jaw dropped so quickly she was pretty sure she had dislocated it.

"What the hell?" she said, looking at her mom.

"Honey, we'll explain later," her mom said. "You said you're here for your sister. Put that face away and go say congratulations."

Joey told her feet to move, but they stayed firmly planted on the metal beneath her. She told her jaw to come back up to its normal position and felt it move a fraction of an inch. It was a start.

"But seriously, what the hell is going on?" Joey said, finally willing her feet to move. She could no longer see Dan and Betty because they were surrounded by other people, which seemed to signal to Joey that Betty had said yes.

She said yes. Dan proposed and she said yes. Joey tried to make these words make sense, but with the whole trying to walk thing, her brain was overloaded. Her Dan had just proposed marriage to her little sister, just like he was supposed to do for her last year. The whole thing looked exactly how she remembered it, except for the tiny detail that she had been the one experiencing it at the time.

"I can't breathe," she said, grabbing her dad's arms as they walked onto the grass.

"You can," he said. "You have no idea how sad they both were when you left last year, sweetie. The fact they got through it together is..."

Whatever it was, it was lost in the cacophony of voices as they got closer to Dan and Betty. Joey had never been one to hide her emotions and realized her safest course of action would be to run again, just like she had last year. She looked to her left and tried to see a path to the parking lot.

"*Jo!*"

It was too late. Betty had appeared from the sea of people and was now hugging her. Tears ran down her cheek. She wasn't sure which sister was crying, but she put her arms around Betty and tried to make words come out of her mouth.

"Betty!" she whispered, stroking her sister's hair. "I'm so happy for you."

"Did you see?" Betty pulled back and thrust her left hand into

Joey's face. "I'm getting married!"

"I can't believe it!" Joey said, hoping saying something true would come across as sincere.

Joey looked for Dan and saw him hugging her parents, who once again must have been in on it. And why wouldn't they be? Dan was a perfect son-in-law and now they at least still got to have him in that capacity.

Before Joey could ask one of the millions of questions that had just floated to the front of her brain, Betty was swept away by friends who had heard the news and wanted to see the ring. The same exact ring Joey knew had been meant for her. She'd gotten a good look at it and her heart sank. That ring was sacred, and now it sat on her sister's finger.

Her sister who had kept a letter from her. Wasn't this whole thing Betty's fault? If not for Betty, Joey would have come back to this timeline a year ago and...what, exactly? If coming back in time was her chance to see what her life could have been like with someone else, hadn't this all worked out as it was supposed to? Was this the answer to all her problems?

Dan and Betty would be happy together. Probably. Joey couldn't picture it, but she also didn't know how much the two of them had changed in her absence. Original timeline Dan and Betty were always meant to be siblings, of that she was sure. Betty was too unpredictable for sensible, steady Dan. If anything, Dan seemed even less suited for Betty in this world.

But was Betty somehow more suited for Dan now? She *had* seemed a bit more mature in their phone chats. But even a more mature Betty still seemed so very wrong with her Dan. She realized with a pang in her chest she'd better stop thinking of him that way.

Joey reached her hands to her face to check that she was, in fact, smiling. She knew anyone who knew her would be able to tell it was a fake smile, but it felt better than the shocked looked she was wearing on the inside. And the tears on her cheeks could easily be explained because she was happy for her sister. And her friend, Dan.

She reached into her purse and felt the paper with Mary Fate's address on it and wondered if it was time to undo everything, assuming that was still an option. But as she looked at Betty and Dan, reunited after accepting dozens of well wishes, she let the paper go and vowed to give this new situation a chance. She loved Dan enough to step aside if he was happy.

Now she just had to see for herself if that was really true.

CHAPTER THIRTY

IT ONLY TOOK a day for Joey to realize how awful it feels to be a third wheel. As annoying as Betty had always seemed to her, Joey now understood her frustration.

She didn't forgive her or anything, but she understood. The whole family was thrilled with the engagement and immediately fell into wedding planning mode. Joey shouldn't have been surprised because they'd done the same thing for her, but from the outside, it suddenly felt really annoying.

If she had hoped to avoid the arrangements, those hopes were immediately dashed when Betty woke her up the next morning and invited her to breakfast.

"Come on," she said, sitting on the foot of Joey's bed. "My

treat."

Not one to turn down free breakfast, Joey pulled herself out of bed and took in her appearance in her dresser mirror. She was terribly jetlagged and had barely slept all night. Everything was fuzzy, and she looked about as good as she felt. No wonder Dan wanted to marry Betty. She was a hot mess.

Betty drove them to their favorite place for waffles and rattled on about everything Joey had missed while she was away.

"And don't worry, Dad filmed it, so I can show you later," she said, ending her story about the school musical.

As they walked into the restaurant, Joey turned to her sister and came to a halt.

"You're leaving a few things out," she said. "Or at least, a certain someone."

Betty blushed and cast her eyes down. "Oh, Jo," she said. "Can you ever forgive me?"

Joey knew the only way forward was to accept this new reality. And so she lied.

"There's nothing to forgive. I just want to hear how it all happened."

"Really?" Betty looked back up. "Oh, Joey! You're the best! I was going to wait until we were seated, but would you be my maid of honor?"

Since she was apparently no longer saying true things anymore, she heard the words "I'd love to," come out of her mouth.

Betty squealed and hugged her, then pulled her inside. As they sat, Betty started from the beginning.

"Well, he was just so sad after you left," she began. "We all were. But he took it really hard. His dad got him that job to keep him busy, but everyone was really worried about him. I think he just doesn't do well with surprises."

Joey tried not to roll her eyes. Betty was erasing how Dan felt about Joey from this story. It was probably what she told herself so much she actually started to believe it.

"Anyway, we started hanging out a bit and got really close. I realized he had feelings for me, and I tried to tell him I didn't feel that way about him, Joey. I really did."

Joey knew this wasn't true but nodded.

"But, well, he asked me out on a date, and I thought I should at least see how it felt. And then I knew I couldn't just be friends with him anymore. He said he never really loved you and knew it was supposed to be me all along. I never realized it, but that's exactly how I felt too."

Joey was thankful she had a mouthful of waffle, because it was the only thing that kept her from yelling. Or maybe crying. But she sat there and chewed and thought about what she was hearing. Betty had a tendency to gloss over things in her stories, but she had never really lied about something with Joey before. At least, Joey didn't think she had.

If Dan had told Betty he'd always been in love with her, what else could she do but stand aside? Maybe he'd settled for her all along and had been pining for Betty in those months leading up to the end, finally realizing he'd married the wrong sister.

"Betty, can I ask you something?" Joey said.

"Of course," Betty said.

"Why did you hide my scholarship letter?"

"Oh, I didn't know you knew about that," she said. "But, I mean, you got there, and it all worked out, right?"

"No, Betty. I mean, yes, I did still go there, but that doesn't mean hiding the letter was okay."

"Okay. But you have to understand. I was *so* mad at you."

"When?"

"So, remember when I wanted to go to Dan's prom? Well, I called that guy Trent from his school who went to camp with us and asked if he'd go with me. None of Dan's friends had called and I was getting desperate. Well, Trent said you told him I couldn't go to the prom, so he'd asked someone else."

Joey felt herself deflate.

"Betty, I'm sorry. I really shouldn't have done that. I just...you know what? I'm not going to offer excuses. I shouldn't have done that."

"I know. That was so mean. Anyway, I hung up with Trent and was looking for a way to get back at you. I was in your room when Dan stopped by with the letter. He put it on your desk. He looked so sad. So, I decided getting rid of the letter would make

Dan happy and be a less permanent revenge. How could you be mad at losing something you never knew you had?"

Joey looked at her sister. Was this how she had been at eighteen? It was impossible to see herself clearly in hindsight, but she knew on some level they were similar. Could she have done something to deliberately hurt someone she loved, just out of spite?

The answer came to her like a bolt of lightning. She already had. She was mad at Dan about the letter, but instead of talking to him about it, she ran away. Instead of just asking him to put off proposing while she went to London, she had taken off, leaving him behind to pick up the pieces of the life he had planned.

Leaving him to fall into the arms of her sister. He was better than the two of them put together. Joey still wasn't sure whether Betty and Dan belonged together, but she no longer knew whether she and Dan did either.

Had she ever deserved him?

CHAPTER THIRTY-ONE

AFTER BREAKFAST, JOEY called Taylor to let her know she'd arrived safely and fill her in on what was going on.

"Not dead?" Taylor said as she answered the phone.

"Sorry," Joey said. "I should have called as soon as I landed. You wouldn't believe everything that's happened since I got here."

"I could say the same. Want to go first?"

"No. What's up?"

"Well, I've been offered a spot in the National Orchestra."

"You what? That's amazing!"

"I know! I can't believe it," Taylor gushed. "It's with the local portion that plays in and around London so I can keep going to school. But if things go well, I could join the touring group once I graduate."

Joey was so relieved. She wasn't sure this was exactly how Taylor's life had gone before, but she knew this was a huge opportunity and was thankful she hadn't knocked her completely off course.

"So, basically, it also means I can move off campus," Taylor continued. "But we can talk about that when you come back."

"Ah, yeah, about that," Joey said. "I'm not sure when I'll be coming back."

"Did you and Dan..."

"No. No, no. He actually proposed to Betty last night."

"He *what?*"

Joey filled Taylor in on everything that had happened since she landed.

"Wow," Taylor said. "How do you feel about all of that?"

"Honestly, I'm not sure," Joey said. "I want them both to be happy. I'm just not sure they will be happy together."

"Yeah. I can see that."

"So, I guess wedding plans are full steam ahead, and since I'm maid of honor, I was thinking I should hang here for a while to help."

"Of course. Well, I'm here if you need me. I'm always here, Joey."

Joey whispered, "Thanks, bye," before hanging up. Speaking of people she didn't deserve, could Taylor have been more understanding? And not just now, but about everything. Joey had come crashing into her life one year ago and Taylor had never, not once, made her feel anything but welcome. Even now, after she'd embarrassed herself by almost proposing, Taylor wanted her to be okay with this news.

And so, Joey kicked off Operation Dan and Betty. She'd been in a few weddings and always took her role in the bridal party seriously. You don't stand up and vouch for just anyone. She had just agreed to be Betty's maid of honor. Everything that happened before and between the three of them was irrelevant. And if her sister was getting married, she knew it was up to her to make sure the guy was worthy.

"Hello, Daniel," she said when he picked up the phone.

"Hello JoEllen," he said.

"I hate when you use my full name."

"You started it," Dan laughed. "What's up?"

"Well, since you are marrying my sister, I thought I should get to know you."

"You've known me forever, weirdo."

"Yes, but that was before. I'd like to get to know this new Dan and see what my new brother-in-law will be like. Want to meet up later?"

"That sounds like a date," he said quietly.

"No, er..." she replied. He was right. She couldn't just go out alone with him like they used to. "I mean with Betty. We can go out together."

And thus, her stint as a third wheel began. They decided dinner together would be nice and Joey let Dan call his fiancée to propose the idea.

"Hey!" Betty said, appearing at the door to Joey's bedroom a few minutes later. "You, me, Dan, dinner?"

"Sounds perfect," Joey said before Betty could bounce away.

Joey unpacked her suitcase and sighed when her hand touched the ring box from the antique store. She opened it and stared at it for a minute before deciding it was too pretty to sit in the dark. And since she was about to be out with Dan and Betty, a little something sparkly to grab on to when she felt nervous seemed like the perfect totem to keep herself calm.

She lay down on her bed to rest a bit to try to clear the jetlag from her brain, but accidentally fell asleep. When she woke up, she saw she only had ten minutes to get ready. She hadn't packed much because she figured she could just wear her old clothes, but quickly realized they no longer fit. And thus, she wore jeans and a sweater to dinner on a day when most people were in shorts and T-shirts.

She heard the front door open and knew Dan was there to pick them up. He'd long since forgone the hassle of ringing their doorbell or knocking, but Joey thought that was just for her. Apparently in her absence, he'd extended the same level of casual dating technique to Betty.

But when she came out of her room to say hi, she realized the casual vibe ended with his entrance. Dan was dressed in slacks and a collared shirt, something he rarely did when he and Joey went out, especially at this age. He must have seen the look she gave him because he looked down sheepishly and said, "Oh, yeah, Betty prefers this."

Of course she did. Where Joey had liked going on cheap dates with Dan, even sometimes competing for who could find the least expensive outings, Betty preferred her dates a little fancier.

A lot fancier, actually. When Betty came out in a new dress she'd apparently shopped for while Joey napped, Dan's reaction was subtle, but Joey saw it. He immediately stood up a little straighter and quickly told Betty how pretty she looked.

He's uncomfortable, she realized. He didn't look unhappy, per se, but he definitely wasn't at ease around Betty the way he'd always been with her. Betty liked things to be a certain way and in Joey's absence had molded Dan into the version of him she preferred. His new car suddenly made more sense. It wasn't like him to splurge on something like that, even if he did have the money.

But Betty wouldn't have been caught dead in his old car and had likely told him so.

Joey knew this wasn't the Dan she'd left behind and felt immediately protective. She reminded herself to give them a chance before judging. Sure, she could tell Dan was uncomfortable, but maybe he just still got butterflies around Betty in a way he hadn't with her. That could be a thing, right?

"Dan, I thought I told you not to wear that belt with those

shoes," Betty said, by way of greeting.

Dan looked down, clearly embarrassed, and Joey's heart sank.

Strike one, Betty, she thought as she followed them out of the house. She wasn't sure what she'd do if Betty amassed three strikes, but she was keeping score in the meantime.

CHAPTER THIRTY-TWO

BY THE TIME they got to the restaurant, Betty had basically struck out, as far as Joey was concerned.

"I'm not saying I don't like it," she said during the drive. "I'm just saying I think we should pick something out that's a little more *me.*"

She'd been engaged fewer than twenty-four hours and was already complaining about her engagement ring. Joey had to bite her tongue in the backseat. How could she not like that ring? Joey had loved that ring. It was white gold with a single, round diamond. Not too fancy, but so sweet and so Dan. Granted, it did seem odd that he hadn't gotten Betty her own ring, but maybe it had been too late to return it.

"I thought maybe we could get something a little bigger for an anniversary one day," Dan said.

Joey wanted to cry. He had said those same words to her before their tenth anniversary. But she had loved the ring too much to even think about trading it in. And here was her sister, ready to throw it away like a Cracker Jack toy.

"Oh, that's so sweet," Betty said. "You're right. We should save your money for Europe, anyway."

"Europe?" Joey asked.

"Oh, didn't we tell you?" Betty said. "Dan's going to take a year off from school so we can have, like, this year-long honeymoon."

Joey caught Dan's eye in the rearview mirror and tried to convey her reaction to the news.

Are you kidding me? What about saving up and finishing school early? Won't you lose your scholarship? Who even are you?

If Dan could hear her inner monologue, he didn't react. But Joey was livid. Betty was moving on with the life she'd planned, but this time bringing Dan along to be her sidekick. She knew Betty's Europe trip was a blur of parties, drugs, sex, and odd jobs here and there to pay her way through. She'd spent a month in Ibiza as a waitress and told Joey she "wouldn't believe" everything she did there. Joey didn't ask.

And she didn't judge her sister for any of it, back then. They were two really different people and where Joey found comfort in familiarity, Betty was always searching for the next big thing.

How could Dan love such different people? Had he built the life they had together because he wanted it, or because he thought she did? What if they had talked more before their wedding and discovered that they both wanted to experience more before settling down. Not like Betty, but maybe a study abroad program? They'd talked about it, but then Joey got pregnant and traveling became a "maybe once the kids are grown" thing.

"Wow," Joey said. "I think that sounds amazing."

Dan furrowed his brow. Just like she could tell he was miserable, but too afraid to speak up, he could tell she was lying. It was weird that Betty couldn't, but Joey chalked it up to Betty's selective remembering. She could hear what she wanted from the people around her in real time, just as easily as she could play it back after the fact to look how she wanted it.

Well, Joey couldn't and as she pretended to read her menu, she tried to think through a game plan. First, she had to talk to Dan alone again. Going somewhere together alone was definitely inappropriate, but she'd have to come up with an excuse to get him on his own. Maybe she could suggest that she help him shop for an engagement gift for Betty? It wasn't something she'd expected when she was engaged, but she had a feeling it was exactly the kind of thing Betty wouldn't mention but would be secretly pissed he hadn't done.

Okay, so she could get him alone, but what would she say?

She glanced over at him, sitting next to Betty and looking so stiff she wanted to cry for him. That's what she'd say. She could tell him, as a friend, that he seemed uncomfortable around the person he should be most comfortable with. Maybe she was reading the situation wrong. That would give him a chance to explain it to her.

Betty was beautiful and enigmatic and impossible to ignore. Maybe he really had been in love with her the whole time but intimidated by her then and still. Joey was always the more approachable sister. She knew she was pretty, but not Betty-pretty. And she was so focused on school that she knew she could sometimes be a little nerdy.

Okay, a lot nerdy. But so was Dan. A lump formed in Joey's throat as she thought through all the things he'd miss if he married Betty. Dressing up for midnight book releases when new Harry Potter books came out (Betty wouldn't have been caught dead). Costume parties with friends on days other than Halloween. Hosting a party for the finale of *Game of Thrones*. Then being *really* mad at the end of *Game of Thrones* for weeks. Okay, years.

Wouldn't he miss all of that? Or had he only ever done those things because Joey had wanted to? She tried to imagine Dan in a nightclub in Spain and couldn't picture it. They enjoyed a drink every once in a while and tried pot when it was legal, but never anything on the level Joey knew Betty was about to. Or what she assumed, anyway.

Dan, in his cargo shorts and T-shirts, with a backward baseball hat, just didn't belong anywhere other than with her. Betty could dress him up however she wanted to, but new clothes didn't mean a damn thing.

"So, Joey," Betty said after they'd ordered. "Tell us about London."

"Oh." Joey tried to relax her face so they wouldn't see how focused she'd been on Dan.

"Have you written anything?" Dan asked.

"Quite a bit, actually," Joey said. "I've written five novels. Almost six."

She tried not to outwardly wince at the thought of that sixth manuscript, still unfinished.

"That's incredible," said Dan. "Can we read them?"

"Oh yeah, can we?" Betty asked.

Joey smiled and let herself fall into easy conversation with Betty and Dan about everything she'd written, and the things she'd seen while she was away. She knew they both would be so excited and supportive of her writing, and it felt good to ease her scrutiny of them as a couple for a bit and just enjoy them as people.

She told them about Liam and Will and their trips to Cornwall and even Paris. She told them she'd made a bet that the Angels would win the World Series and it had paid off big.

"How big?" Betty asked.

"Oh, like a hundred quid," she said, realizing she didn't want to share the actual number with her sister.

"So you bet, what, one pound?" Dan said. "Wouldn't there have been like one hundred to one odds when you did it?"

Damn. He was good.

"Something like that," Joey said, brushing it off. "Anyway, we saw all the sights and went to a few plays. London is basically the greatest city in the world."

"Yeah, if you're boring," Betty said.

Joey bristled, but she knew it wouldn't sound appealing the way she was telling it. Not to her sister, anyway.

"It sounds amazing," Dan said.

Joey smiled and couldn't help but think of how they'd always dreamed of going to London someday. In fact, they were saving to go in two years, before everything had changed.

"Well, of course it does." Betty put her arm around Dan and kissed his cheek. "We'll definitely stop by on the honeymoon. But we'll see all the fun stuff that Joey missed."

The food arrived at that exact moment, saving Joey from saying something she might regret. And besides, she had plenty of time to get to the bottom of this relationship. But from what she'd seen so far, Operation Dan and Betty felt more like a rescue mission than reconnaissance.

And she didn't plan to leave her man behind.

CHAPTER THIRTY-THREE

"A MONTH?" JOEY said the next morning. "You're getting married in a month?"

"Why not?" Betty said, sitting across from her at the kitchen table. They were both still in pajamas and Betty was eating Lucky Charms. She did not look like someone who was ready to get married in a month.

"No reason," Joey said. "You're right. I can't think of a single reason why you shouldn't get married in a month."

Sarcasm was lost on Betty, so Joey rolled her eyes and changed the subject.

"I was thinking of seeing if Dan wants to go shopping with me," she said.

"Just the two of you?" Betty said as a drop of milk rolled down her chin.

"Well, I'm not sure he knows he's supposed to get you an engagement gift, and I thought he could use some help."

"Oh!" Betty clapped. "You're a lifesaver. I keep dropping hints, but he's basically the worst gift-giver ever."

Joey wanted to smack her sister. Dan was most certainly not a bad gift-giver. He just probably didn't spend nearly enough on Betty for her liking. When she wasn't being critical, she could see how Dan had fallen for Betty while she was gone. But how had Betty fallen for Dan?

Joey thought back on where Betty would be right about now in her regular timeline. She had spent her senior year single, but accepted dates from all the cutest boys at their high school and several surrounding ones. She had attended seven proms and would have gone to more if some hadn't fallen on the same night. She had insisted that each of her dates buy her a dress for the occasion and each one had jumped at the chance to do it. Most of them even paid for her to have her hair and makeup done.

Without all those suitors, Dan must have taken up the brunt of everything Betty asked for. And since her heart had always been set on a trip to Europe after high school, Dan had had no choice but to go along. He probably proposed so he'd be able to lock her down before she decided to go away without him. Not a bad strategy, but she had countered with a quick wedding.

Joey reached for the notepad sitting between them on the table where Betty and Dan had been making notes after dinner last night.

"Uh, Betty?"

"Yeah?"

"Aren't these the same ideas you had for your sweet sixteen party?" Joey said.

"I didn't have a sweet sixteen party," Betty said with an edge of annoyance in her voice.

Joey knew very well that she didn't have that party. Years before, she had tried to convert to Judaism, saying it was because she felt called to do so, but their mom and dad correctly guessed that she just wanted a Bat Mitzvah. Then, she had asked why only her Hispanic friends got to have a quinceañera. Then, she had come to them with a Power Point presentation about how a "Super Sweet Sixteen" party would be a good investment.

Her parents hadn't fallen for it, but apparently Dan had, on some level. The notepad was full of Betty's handwriting with what looked to be exactly what she'd listed in that presentation, even down to the same DJ. She had to hand it to her: when Betty made her mind up about something, she usually got it.

After breakfast, Joey called Dan and asked if she could help him shop.

"Uh, isn't the ring an engagement gift?" he said.

"You'd think so," Joey said. "I mean, yeah, but I thought you might want to get her something else."

"Oh, yeah, sure."

They made a plan to head to Scottsdale Fashion Square in a few hours, so Joey had time to sit with Betty and look through the bridal magazines she'd picked up. Joey recognized them all as the same ones she had pored over when she planned her own wedding. Hers wasn't nearly as fancy as what Betty was planning, but she did manage to replicate lots of the ideas in those magazines with some DIY gusto and help from friends.

Then she saw it. The dress she'd fallen in love with nineteen years ago. She stared at the page and traced the satin bodice with her fingers. She'd found a local dress shop that carried it back then and stupidly tried it on, hoping it wouldn't look good on her. It did. But it also had a $2000 price tag and there was no way she could afford it. Instead, she talked to the home-ec teacher at Conquistador and asked if she could help her make something similar.

Looking at the picture now, Joey laughed a bit realizing how much they'd missed the mark. The shape was similar, but the hems were a little crooked and the material wasn't as shiny. It hadn't mattered to her then and it certainly didn't now, but she suddenly felt like crying, wondering if she'd ever see that dress again.

"Tacky," Betty said, looking over her shoulder.

Okay, now she really might smack her. Betty had gushed when she'd seen Joey on her wedding day, but Joey had always secretly wondered if she really liked the dress. She had her answer.

"I think it looks nice," Joey said.

"Oh, I mean, yeah." Betty looked at it again. "It would look really nice for like a country wedding or something. But I want something more dramatic."

Of course you do. Joey flipped the page.

They dog-eared a few of the ones Betty wanted to try on and Joey promised to call a few shops to set up appointments for the next day. Betty was antsy about buying off-the-rack, but Joey assured her she'd look gorgeous in a potato sack and meant it, kissing her cheek as she left to go meet Dan.

He was walking up as she walked out, and Joey wanted to run up and hug him as soon as she saw him. He wasn't wearing cargo shorts, but the rest was the Dan she knew. Apparently, he was still in there somewhere, just hiding from Betty.

"There you are," she said.

"Here I am," he replied.

"No, I mean there *you* are," she said. "The real you. Not Dan Dan the fancy man."

He tried to look annoyed, but Joey knew she'd gotten through to him. He couldn't pretend around her.

And now she had him alone, she was going to find out why he was even trying.

CHAPTER THIRTY-FOUR

"SO, FANCY CAR, fancy new clothes," Joey said as she buckled her seatbelt.

"You keep using that word," he said. "I do not think it means what you think it means."

They both laughed, and Joey relaxed at the sound of Dan's genuine, actual chuckle. Maybe this wouldn't be as hard as she thought.

"So, an engagement gift," he said as they pulled away from his driveway. "Please tell me what I'm supposed to be looking for here?"

"No idea," Joey said. "But we'll know it when we see it."

"Fair enough." He shrugged.

He turned on the radio to fill the silence, but music had always been their thing, and it only took one song for them to hear one that held a special meaning.

"I can just..." Dan said, reaching down to turn it off.

"No, let it play," she said, falling just short of touching his hand to stop him.

"From This Moment On" by Shania Twain had been a favorite song for them to sing together, and he'd surprised Joey with tickets to see her in concert a few years back. He didn't know it, but it would also end up being the first song on the wedding soundtrack they'd given out as favors for their reception. Or, knowing Dan, he did know because it had been his idea and he might have had it before he proposed.

They listened to it and Joey wondered what songs he and Betty had landed on in the past year. She couldn't bear the thought of him using any of the ones that had been theirs, but she was also sure it wouldn't be an issue. Betty was aware of the songs that belonged to Dan and Joey. She'd never have agreed to a secondhand song.

"You seem more relaxed today," Joey said as the song ended.

"Relaxed?" Dan said.

"Yeah, maybe that's not the right word. I got the feeling last night like you were nervous."

"I'm not nervous around you." He sounded defensive.

"I didn't mean around me."

"Betty? Why would I be nervous around Betty?"

"Because she dresses you and tells you how to stand and sit. And you want to make her happy."

She added that last part so it didn't sound so accusatory. If she tried too much too soon, Dan would shut down and the whole day would be a waste.

"Yeah, well, you know Betty," he said. "And yes, I do want to make her happy. Is that a bad thing?"

"Not at all," Joey said. "I want you to make her happy too."

"You do?"

"I want you both to be happy together." It sounded weird to say out loud on a day when she was actively trying to break them up, but assuming she failed, she knew that was, in fact, the goal.

"Oh. Well, thank you."

"Can I ask about the honeymoon?"

"I knew you had a problem with that," Dan said.

"So, you did hear me?" Joey laughed.

"Well, you were shouting with your expression." He joined her laugh. He had told her for years she had no poker face, but it was worse than that. If she was mad, everyone who could see her face would immediately know. She was tactful and kind, but her face gave her away every time.

"What about your scholarship?" she continued. If the topic was on the table, she was going to see how much she could get out of him.

"Deferred," he said. "You're allowed to do that for up to one year before you start, so I requested an exception and they granted it."

"And what about graduating early?"

"I'll see the world and learn plenty on our trip. Isn't that better than finishing my degree a little early?"

That was Betty talking through him and she knew it. Dan had worn his early graduation status like a badge of honor, and she knew why. He'd worked his butt off to do it and it had always been a goal. Betty's logic wasn't terrible, but it wasn't Dan.

"So, I guess you've thought of everything," she said. "And you really want to go?"

Dan hesitated and Joey waited patiently to give him time to think.

"If you'd asked me a year ago, I would have said no," he said finally. "But I think I really do now. And it's kinda your fault."

"My fault?"

"Seeing you run away last year really changed me. I was so sure of what our, er, my future would look like that it never occurred to me to think about other options. But you leaving made me realize there are paths other than the straight and narrow."

"But you like the straight and narrow."

"So did you," Dan said quietly. "Or so I thought."

"I still do. I thought I wanted something else, but this year has taught me that the life I was running away from was actually perfect."

Dan flinched. She'd gone too far. It was cruel to say that to the guy she'd left behind.

"Well, maybe I need to experience that year away so I can come to the same conclusion."

There. That's what this all came down to. She'd run away and now he was going to too. It wasn't out of spite. If anything, it was flattery.

"Going to Europe with Betty isn't going to be at all like my year away," she said. "You know that, right?"

"Oh hey, look, we're here," he said, turning the car into one of the parking garages.

Joey left that last thought dangling in the air as they found a spot and made their way to the entrance. She knew Dan would be thinking about it for the rest of the day.

And she knew better than most how a single thought can change your fate.

CHAPTER THIRTY-FIVE

"SO, DO WE just wander, or did you have a place in mind?" Dan said as they looked up and around to get their bearings. They had both worked here during college, so she knew the place pretty well, but since she had no reason to know it well in her current timeline, she figured she should just play dumb. Besides, wandering would lead to more chatting.

"Uh, how about we fuel up first?" she said, pointing to the food court.

Without asking where he'd want to eat, Joey led them straight to Johnny Rockets.

"Milkshakes and fries?" she said, gesturing to two open seats at the counter.

"Do you even have to ask?" he said, gesturing for her to be seated first.

This had been their favorite place to meet when their breaks lined up during their work schedules. Usually, they'd share one milkshake and order of fries, but that felt too much like a date, so Joey ordered her own.

"So, can I ask *you* something?" Dan said as they waited for their order.

Joey had been asking all the questions, so this seemed fair, but she was worried he'd lead them away from the topics she wanted to focus on.

"Sure," she said.

"Was it just the letter? That made you leave, I mean?"

"Basically." It was impossible for her to say what else had inspired her abrupt change of heart without sounding like a crazy person who believed she had traveled back in time.

"When did you find out about it?" he said.

"The morning of my graduation," she replied.

His face twisted into a pained expression, and she wanted nothing more than to reach out and touch him. Luckily, her milkshake appeared at that same instant and she put her hands to work shoveling the chocolaty goodness into her mouth.

"So, it took you less than a day to decide to leave?" he said. "That actually makes me feel better. I thought you'd been planning it for a while and just didn't tell me."

"Of course not," she said. "Oh Dan, I'm so sorry. I never thought you'd think of it that way. I didn't talk to you about it because I didn't trust myself to go if I stopped too long to think."

He nodded and ate a French fry, but she could see he was still thinking about it.

"And I was too ashamed to face you," she said. "Or angry. I was angry because I thought you'd tried to keep me from my dreams, and ashamed that I couldn't talk to you about it."

"I would have gone with you," he said.

It was easy for him to say that in hindsight, but Joey wondered if it was the truth. Could there have been a hidden option C where they got to experience that life together before building the one they eventually did? It certainly felt like a nice compromise for them both, but she'd never know how that would all play out.

But maybe there was a way for him to know how their life could have been, and maybe could still be. She wasn't ready to play her final card yet, but Joey knew if all else failed, she could try to tell Dan all about the timeline she'd already lived. If he couldn't see that Betty was wrong for him, she'd have to show him how right she was.

"So, engagement present," he said after a minute or so of awkward silence.

"Yes, what's your budget?" Joey said, turning to face him.

"Uh, I don't have one?"

"No wonder she loves you!" Joey gave him a sisterly punch in the arm.

"I mean, I wasn't thinking about how much to spend. We're not going to go crazy, are we?"

"Maybe we'll get lucky and find something that looks really expensive but is on sale." Joey did her best to sound encouraging.

"That would be great." Dan stood up.

They headed away from the food court and Joey pretended to not know what each store had in it, so they ended up stopping in a lot of stores that made no sense for their mission. Joey was pretty sure she knew where they'd end up, but she wanted to keep Dan out and occupied for as long as she could.

They didn't talk about Betty much, other than the occasional "do you think she'd like this?"

They did talk about the books Joey had written and Dan made her stop a few times during her explanations so she wouldn't spoil the endings for him.

"You really want to read my books?" she said as they walked out of a store that only sold men's clothes. Oops.

"Of course I do," he said as they continued on their way.

"You just never seemed that interested before." Joey realized a second too late that this made no sense.

"When have you written a book before?"

"Oh, er, I mean," she stammered, unable to think of a sensible-sounding reply. "I just always assumed you wouldn't be all that interested in reading what I wrote."

It was true, in a way. Even when she was able to find time to write while they were married, it took him weeks, sometimes even months to get around to reading what she sent him. And if she couldn't get her own husband to read what she wrote, how was she ever going to convince strangers to buy her books?

She remembered with a jolt a particularly painful conversation they'd had when the kids were little. Their youngest was in kindergarten and she finally had a few hours each day where she could find time to write. And since she was used to having very little time, she discovered she was a pretty fast writer.

"And so I was thinking," she said one night as they climbed into bed. "If I can just write, like, ten books a year and figure out how to publish them myself, maybe I could build a following. And maybe by the time we retire, I could make a million dollars!"

Dan had laughed. Scoffed, really.

"What?" she said. "Don't you think I'm a good writer?"

"Sure," he said. "I just don't think you're going to make a million dollars as one."

She felt like a really full balloon that had come untied and bounced around the room as it deflated. She had been researching self-publishing for months and trying to learn as much as she could. She didn't think she'd ever make it big, but with enough books and enough time, it didn't seem that far-fetched.

But if the person who was supposed to believe in her more than anyone else in the world didn't think she could do it, how did she ever expect to actually do it?

And yet, here he was, clearly interested and engaged with her stories now. Had a decade of work and kids jaded him to the point where he no longer believed in her? Or had this year apart made him realize he took her for granted?

And did any of that matter when she was a month away from losing him forever?

CHAPTER THIRTY-SIX

"I HAVE TO get out of this mall," Dan said as they stood in the Louis Vuitton store.

"What's wrong?" she whispered.

"That bag," he said, pointing to a case in the wall, "costs more than Betty's engagement ring."

Joey tried to stifle her laugh as they walked out but failed and was hit with a nasty look from a very annoyed looking store employee.

"Okay, okay," Joey said once they were out of earshot. "But there are other nice purses you don't have to go into debt for."

"I dunno," Dan said. They'd been shopping for hours, and the milkshake burst of energy had long since worn off. Joey couldn't believe he'd hung in there for so long. He either really wanted to please Betty or was afraid to piss her off.

Or maybe he was enjoying the time with Joey. She hoped that was it but didn't want to jinx it. They were getting close to the store she knew would be the winner but wasn't quite ready to take him there.

"Can we at least sit down for a bit?" he said. "I think I got something in my shoe when we were in that bead store."

"Sure," she said, turning to the left.

"Food court is back that way," he pointed out.

"Yeah, but I feel like there's some place to sit up this way." She led them to the Pottery Barn and pretended to find it as they approached.

"Sit?" he said.

"Couches," she said.

"Ahh." He nodded, following her inside.

Dan collapsed into the first couch they saw as only a man who is being dragged around a mall by a woman can.

"Tired, Grandpa?" she said, laughing as he leaned back into the cushy upholstery.

"Mentally, yes," he said. "Do you think Betty would like this couch?"

He laughed, but it reminded her of the first couch they bought together and she welled up.

When the hand-me-down couch they'd been given from her

aunt had become too uncomfortable to sit on any longer, she and Dan had walked into The Room Store one Labor Day weekend, armed with an ad they'd seen in the Sunday *Arizona Republic*.

"We'd like this couch," Joey had announced to the first salesperson who approached them.

"Oh, well, we don't have that one in stock," he said. "But I do have some nice other ones over here if you'll just follow me."

"Sir, we want the $200 couch in this ad," Dan said. "Do any other stores have it in stock?"

"I'd have to call," he said. "But may I show you what we do have in the meantime?"

"We want. The $200. Couch," Joey said. "And we're going to pay in cash. The ad also says no taxes or delivery fees this weekend."

"Oh, uh, I think the fine print lists some exclusions..."

"Sir, my wife here is pregnant. Her back hurts. Our couch at home has fallen apart. We would like this couch that your store is advertising, and we'd like you take this money and our address and make that happen so we can get out of here before her morning sickness kicks back in."

Joey made a face like she might throw up right there on the spot as Dan proffered a stack of mostly tens, fives, and ones.

The salesman took the money and the Post-it note Joey had used to write down their address, came back once to ask what color they'd like, then came back one last time to give them a receipt and delivery information.

And now, here Joey was in a store she'd never been able to afford, joking about buying a $3000 couch for her sister. She suddenly wanted to leave even more than she knew Dan did.

"I have an idea," she said. "And if you like it, we can be out of here in ten minutes."

"Deal," Dan said, hopping up like a spring chicken.

She no longer pretended that she didn't know where she was going and led him straight to Tiffany & Co.

"I know I said no budget, but..." He stared up at the intimidating signage.

"There are some things here that aren't too bad," she said.

They walked in and Joey asked the salesperson who greeted them to take them to the Elsa Perretti section. She was young and pretty and probably annoyed by two teenagers coming in and asking for some of the least expensive items they sold, but she was courteous and Joey realized she was probably just projecting.

"Did you have something specific in mind?" she said, showing them to the case.

"It's for my sister," Joey said. "An engagement gift from her new fiancé here."

"How sweet," the salesperson said. Joey had definitely been projecting. She looked at the woman's nametag. Tiffany was her name, and Joey felt herself willing Dan to not make a Tiffany working at Tiffany's joke. Or had he only developed that impulse after they'd had kids?

Joey pointed at the letter necklaces she thought Betty might like. Each one had a single, cursive letter on it. Joey knew Betty liked it because she'd always complimented the one Joey got the day she became a mother.

"Should we get her a B for Betty?" Dan said.

"Oh, I was thinking a D for Dan," Joey said. It's what she would have wanted. She eventually had one for each of her kids and loved reaching up to touch them during the day.

"I'm not sure she'd want it to be for my name," Dan said.

It was such a short sentence, but it was charged with so much emotion. Dan doubted Betty's love for him just like Joey did.

"I mean, the B is prettier," he said, realizing what he'd just implied.

"And if it flips, it looks just like the D," Tiffany said helpfully.

That settled it. Dan bought the B and Joey knew exactly how big Betty's eyes would get when she saw the little blue box it came in.

They walked to the car together in companionable silence. The day had been a success, and not just because they'd found the perfect gift.

But because she had an idea that might fix everything.

CHAPTER THIRTY-SEVEN

MARY FATE'S "OFFICE" turned out to be a tiny house in an older neighborhood where Joey imagined Mary still lived with her parents. Joey had borrowed her mom's car and said she'd meet everyone at the first bridal shop, but that she had to run an errand first. Dan had left the Tiffany's box with her with special instructions to present it when she found her dress. He'd included a note inside, but Joey wasn't supposed to read it.

And she wouldn't. Probably.

But before she could go sit and watch her sister try on dozens of expensive dresses, she decided to pay a visit to the woman who had turned her life upside-down. She walked up to the door and knocked three times.

A nice-looking man about her dad's age answered and invited her in when she said she was there to see Mary.

"Mary!" he called. "Company!"

And a minute later, there she was. Twenty years younger, but definitely the same person she'd met in that gymnasium.

"Hi," she said. "Do I know you?"

Mary's dad eyed Joey suspiciously and waited to see how things played out.

"I'm Joey," she said. "We met at an event. You were telling fortunes? I found you online and I'm sorry to just show up like this, but I'm hosting a party next week and wanted to hire you."

"Oh!" Mary said excitedly. "Were you at the Schellbachs' anniversary party?"

"Yes!" Joey said. "I know there were a lot of people that night, but I just thought you did a great job and wondered if you would be available for my, uh, reunion."

"Your reunion?" Mary's dad said. "How old are you?"

"My, uh, one-year reunion," Joey said. "It's a new thing we're trying out so that we can stay in touch."

"Oh, well, let me get my calendar," Mary said. "Do you want to come to my room?"

"Sure," Joey said, relieved to be away from Mary's dad.

She followed Mary down the hall and into her room, then nearly fell when Mary closed the door and turned on her.

"Are you here to make fun of me?" she said, inches away from

Joey's nose.

"What? No!" Joey said, leaning back on the dresser she was about to fall on for support.

"I just made the Schellbachs' anniversary party up," Mary said. "So, if you're here because the girls at my school put you up to this, please just leave."

Joey felt awful. Mary's room was covered in dragons, unicorns, crystal balls, fantasy books, and things she couldn't even identify. She was wearing clothes that were no longer in style and had maybe never been in style. She was weird, something Joey appreciated, but she had probably been bullied pretty hard.

"Mary, this is going to sound crazy," Joey began. "But have you been learning about time travel?"

Mary took a step back and cocked her head to the side.

"I wouldn't say learning," she said. "More like, exploring."

"Because you don't just want to tell people's future, right? You want to show them what could have been."

"No, because people in this time suck. I want to go see what other time periods were like."

Joey laughed but stopped when she saw Mary's expression change. "Not laughing at you," she explained, putting her hands up to show she meant no harm. "I'm just pretty sure you're going to master time travel some day and wanted to see if you're already able to do it."

"Who are you?" Mary asked again. "Or should I say, *when*

are you?"

"I'm Joey. And I'm from the year 2022. I think you sent me back here because you thought I married the wrong person. And I'm hoping you can send me back to my timeline or send me back to 2002 so I can have one more chance."

"I sent *you* back in time? Why would I do that? Why am I in 2022 and not some other time..."

The last question was rhetorical, but Joey still felt like answering.

"Maybe you experiment on other people?" she offered.

"I would never," Mary said. "Time travel is dangerous. I would only put others at risk if I had made sure it was safe first, which means I also must have traveled through time at some point."

"Maybe people sucked in other times too?"

"That's what I've been afraid of." Mary reached for a notebook. "Hey, did I happen to say anything to you before I sent you back? It would be really helpful to know what I did so I could replicate it."

"Like how Harry knew he could cast a Patronus because he'd already seen himself do it?"

"Exactly." Mary's face brightened. "Hey, if you're from the future, you know how Harry Potter ends!"

"Can we focus?" It was the only time in Joey's life that she'd ever avoided talking with someone about Harry Potter, but she was cutting it close for Betty's appointment and either needed to time travel or get going.

"Yes, of course. But I'm sorry. I can't help you."

"I was afraid you'd say that."

"But I can read your palm or something if you like?"

"You already have. You said..."

"Sh!" She took Joey's hand. "Let me see."

She looked down, then reached back to her shelf for a different book, flipped to a page toward the back, and looked again.

"Your fate line forks in two different directions," she said. "That must be where I sent you back. Have you fixed whatever it was that I told you to?"

"No, and I've somehow made everything worse," Joey said. "You said I married the wrong person, so I came back to see what my life would be without them. And it's wrong. It's all wrong."

"There's no such thing as the wrong person. There's the person you chose, and then everyone else. But hey—give me your number. If I start to get this whole thing figured out, I'll call you and try to send you back or something."

Joey wondered as she left if she could wait however many years that would take.

It didn't seem like she had any other choice.

Chapter Thirty-Eight

JOEY ARRIVED AT Azteca Bridal just as Betty, her mom, Dan's mom, and the rest of the bridal party were making their way inside.

"You made it!" her mom said, pulling her in for a hug. "Everything okay?"

"Absolutely!" she said with a smile.

"Just hang in there, sweetie." Her mom was clearly not fooled.

"I'm good, really." Joey reached down to squeeze her hand.

Bridal dress shopping with someone who looks good in everything should be easy, but Betty was insanely picky and hated making decisions. When the women who worked there offered the ladies champagne, she reached for a glass without even thinking that she wasn't old enough to drink here.

It helped. And as Betty came out in dress after dress, Joey found herself playing along. She'd watched enough *Say Yes to the Dress* through the years to know how to handle a difficult bride. And so, when Betty started to cry because she thought all the dresses made her thighs look big, Joey decided to step in.

"Betty?" she said, knocking on the fitting room door. "It's Joey. Can I come in?"

The door opened and a flustered employee looked at her, clearly thankful for the help.

"I can get her into the next one," Joey said.

The woman mouthed *thank you* as she grabbed the last three gowns off the floor to hang back up and stepped out.

"Hey, kiddo," Joey said, locking eyes with Betty in the mirror.

"I'm sorry," Betty said, sniffling. "I don't know what's wrong with me."

"It's overwhelming." Joey began to undo the corset of the dress Betty had just rejected.

"It's supposed to be fun."

"And it will be," Joey told her. "You'll know the right dress when you put it on. You won't have any doubts. You'll light up and we'll all see it on your face before we even look at the dress. Here, step out."

Betty did as she was told, and Joey watched as she took a deep breath.

"Let's try this one," Joey said, grabbing the closest one to her.

It had about a hundred buttons down the back, but that would give them more time to talk. "Like I was saying." She pulled the dress over Betty's head and positioned it just right. "You'll know. Just like you did with Dan, right?"

She hadn't meant to say it, but it must have been the champagne. She didn't want to provoke Betty and phrasing it as a question might have seemed like a challenge, so she pretended to be very confused by the buttons and knelt to deal with them.

"Yes," Betty said, either ignoring or rising to the challenge. "Just like Dan."

Joey peeked out from behind the dress to gauge Betty's expression. Where she expected to find defiance, she saw only serenity. It wasn't fair to compare them to what she and Dan had. And it wasn't kind. She didn't know how, but Betty did seem to have fallen for Dan. Even if she was trying to change him and even if she was trying to control him. If Dan didn't want that, he could speak up and say something.

Joey stood back up and kept on buttoning. She realized as she went that she'd never gotten to experience this before. Betty had been the one to dress Joey on her wedding day, but this was the first time she'd ever helped her sister into a bridal gown.

"Are you crying?" Betty asked.

"You're so beautiful," Joey said, and meant it. "And it's not just the dress. You're beautiful, Betty, and I love you so much."

Betty turned and hugged Joey and they both cried before

realizing they were surrounded by thousands of dollars of dresses, and it would probably be bad to get their snot and tears all over them.

"Okay, okay," Joey said. "Let's pull it together here. Now, what do we think of this dress?"

"I feel like a bride," she said. "I think this is it. Give me just a second, though, okay? I want to fix my makeup before I come back out so Mom can take a couple pictures."

Joey nodded and left Betty in the room, staring at her reflection. It was unfortunate that their only time together lately had been under such crazy circumstances. Joey had always found little things about Betty annoying, but the good greatly outweighed the bad. Those habits always seemed to come to the surface around big events, and graduation plus engagement plus whirlwind wedding was the perfect storm. No wonder Joey had been so frustrated with her.

There was the added level of tension because of Dan, but she was only seeing them through the eyes of a person who was looking for reasons why they shouldn't be together. And she knew in the month leading up to her own wedding, she'd probably been a little tough to take.

Granted, that was more to do with the fact she had taken on way too much of the planning herself and had given herself an ulcer in the process, but who had been there to calm her down when Dan showed up to their rehearsal still hungover from his bachelor party the night before? Betty. Who had run interference between the family members who didn't get along, making sure everything went smoothly? Betty.

Who had held her hand just before it was time to walk down the aisle and told her she'd never been more beautiful? Well, that was her dad, but Betty was right there nodding.

She sat back down with the group as they waited for Betty to come out. And Joey was right. Everyone could see by the way she carried herself this was the one. It wasn't Joey's favorite of the day, and she doubted it was even Betty's, but it carried their sisterly love energy and Joey knew that was its own kind of magic.

After everyone celebrated with a toast, Joey pulled the gift from Dan out of her purse.

"Okay, Betty," she said. "I was told to give you this when you found your dress."

A collective "aww" came from the women assembled behind her, then a few "oohs" as everyone registered that signature Tiffany blue.

Betty fanned her face to stop her tears from smudging her newly applied makeup and opened the box. The tiny note inside fell to the ground, and as Joey bent down to pick it up, she felt the mood in the room shift.

"What's wrong, Bets?" Joey's mom said.

"Oh, nothing," she said, trying and failing to mask her initial reaction. "It's just...I thought it would be something else."

"Here," Joey said, handing her the note. "What's wrong?"

She whispered the last part so that only Betty could hear it.

"It's cute," Betty whispered back. "But didn't you hear me say I wanted a bigger ring?"

Who was a spoiled brat who absolutely should not be getting married in a month?

Betty.

CHAPTER THIRTY-NINE

WITH ONLY FOUR weeks until the big day, Joey decided she needed to make one last play, and she needed to do it soon. If it failed, she'd still have time to be the best maid of honor ever. And if it worked, she was pretty sure her family could get at least some of their deposits back.

And so, she'd asked Dan to meet her at their apartment the next day before a work dinner she knew he had to attend. She didn't call it their apartment but gave him the address and said it was important. On her way, she stopped at Target to pick up a blanket, candles, and sandwiches. It had to be just how he'd done it, or she'd never convince him.

She got there fifteen minutes before him, and set everything up, including the CD player she brought from her house, and the mix CD she'd assembled for the occasion, with all the songs she could remember from that night. When she heard footsteps approaching, she pushed play and waited for him to walk in. Then tried to stay calm when he did.

"Thanks for meeting me here," she said.

"How?" Dan said, walking into the living room. "How did you know about this?"

Joey had to pay the apartment complex owner $100 to let her use their apartment for the night, but she remembered he was kinda shady and knew he'd take the bribe. She was just glad no one else was renting it at that moment.

"I want to tell you a story." Joey sat down on the floor, the way they had when Dan had set this same picnic up for her. Dan looked behind him at the door and looked ready to protest but was clearly intrigued. He sat down with her, and she took that as a sign to continue.

"Imagine that I didn't leave last year," she said.

"But you did," he said, a pained expression across his face.

"I know. But you told Betty you never really loved me, and you'd always loved her. I just want to say this all once, and then I'll never say it again. Please...let me get it out."

He looked like he was going to say something before she stopped him with the "please," but on she went.

"Imagine a version of our lives where I didn't leave last year," she said. "You would have proposed to me that night, and I would have said yes. We end up here, in this apartment, where we live during school. We would be married by now and so broke we can barely afford to eat some days, but so in love we don't care. Every day is an adventure because we have each other. And soon, we have not one, not two, but three kids. You are the best daddy in the world, and you love our little family more than you ever dreamed you could."

Joey saw the tears rolling down Dan's face but kept going.

"I know you, Dan. I know you better than anyone and I know you're not happy. And I know I'm the one who made you unhappy. But if you'll let me, I'll spend every day of the rest of my life making it up to you. And even if a day comes where you start to drift away from me, I'll find a way to bring us back together. Because this is it. It's you and me. It has always been you and me."

She stopped talking as "Wouldn't It Be Nice" ended and waited for him to say something. Anything.

"I never said that to Betty," he said at last.

"What?"

"I never told Betty I didn't love you. And I definitely never said I'd always loved her."

"You don't love Betty?" Joey was filled with hope.

"I do. It's just...different. And she was there for me when you left. I didn't think I could ever love someone again, but she told me you kept saying how much better off you were without me. I started to think maybe I had fallen for the wrong sister. But now you're here and I don't know what to think anymore."

"Dan, if you love Betty and want to be with her, just say the word and I'll stand beside you on your wedding day and smile. But if you don't, you need to break it off."

Dan looked around the room and shook his head a few times. Joey knew it had been a low blow to set things up the way he'd done for her on their first night in the apartment, but if she could just unlock the part of his heart that still held space for her, she knew they could get back to where they'd been.

"How do you know about this place? How do you know everything you just said?"

"Because I've already lived it," Joey said. "We've been married for nineteen years. On the night of my twentieth high school reunion, I was sent back in time to see how it would have turned out if I'd ended up with someone else."

Dan stared at her, then frowned.

"Why would you have wanted to see what your life was like with someone else? Assuming what you're saying is true, which I don't believe. But pretending it is, what's so wrong with our life that you had to come back and change things?"

"Something changed that last year. I'm not sure what happened, but I think you stopped loving me."

"Impossible."

"Impossible then, or impossible now?"

Dan stood up and pulled Joey into his arms. "Impossible always," he said into her hair. Then he pulled away for a moment to look at her and kissed her.

They kissed and cried and lost track of time, even forgetting that the rest of the world existed. When they pulled apart, Joey thought she'd never been so happy until she saw the look on Dan's face.

"What's wrong?"

"Betty," he whispered.

Heartbroken, Joey knew her efforts had been too late. Dan might have loved her first, and maybe even more, but he was too honorable to just end things with her sister. She would have loved him even more for it if it didn't mean the end of her chance to be with him.

"You're still going to marry her," she said.

"No, I don't believe he is," came Betty's reply from behind her.

CHAPTER FORTY

"WHAT ARE YOU doing here?" Joey said, pulling herself away from Dan and knocking over one of her candles. She stomped it out before it could catch the blanket on fire.

"Dan said he needed to come up here to check something out for a minute," she said. "But I didn't realize you were the thing he had to check out."

"Betty, I can explain," Joey said.

"Oh, I bet you can," Betty said, storming away from them, before turning on her heel to come back. "You two always do this. You *always* do this to me."

"We always what?" Joey said, unable to compare their current situation to anything that had happened before.

"You always go behind my back and leave me out of everything," she said. "It's Joey and Dan and I'm just an afterthought. Even now we're supposed to be getting *married*, you run back to her. *Her*! The one who left you last year and didn't even care."

"Betty, listen," Joey said. Dan hadn't believed her story about their lives, but since lying and pretending everything was okay clearly wasn't working, she decided to try again.

"Dan and I are supposed to be married. We got married a month ago. We had three kids and you're the best aunt ever. And we're really happy. I just came back in time to, er, see about something."

Betty stopped pacing and stared at her.

"What are you talking about?" she said.

"I know it sounds crazy, but I swear it's true. I'm actually thirty-eight. I was sent back in time by a fortune teller because she said I married the wrong person."

"And who were you supposed to marry?" Betty asked.

"I thought it was Taylor, but I think I was wrong," she said.

"Taylor?" Dan said. "Have you been with Taylor this whole time? Like, been with her been with her?"

Joey turned to face him and nodded.

"You really did cheat on me," Dan said. "Betty said you were with someone else, but I didn't want to believe her."

"We weren't together," Joey said. But then she realized they had never officially broken up. She left, but never ended things.

And she was immediately with Taylor. Wow, no wonder both the people in this apartment with her were looking at her like she was scum.

"Look," she said, trying to regain control over the situation. "I know this all sounds crazy. I know you both have every reason to hate me right now. But I've been watching you both since I came home, and I don't think either of you actually wants to marry the other person. Dan, I'm not saying you should marry me, but well, I mean, I am saying that, but I'm first and foremost saying you shouldn't marry her."

Betty's high-pitched scream echoed off the walls. "This is what I'm talking about!" she said. "You threw him away! You left us both behind without saying anything and now you're back, you come up with some stupid story and tell him he shouldn't marry me."

"Betty, I love you, but you wouldn't be happy with Dan," Joey said. "You can already tell. You guys are great friends, but you just don't want the same things."

"We do!" Betty exclaimed. "We both want to get back at you."

Joey sighed. There it was. She'd wondered how Betty had talked herself into Dan and out of everything she knew she wanted. After her gap year, she came back even more restless than when she left. She moved to New York then LA and always seemed to find her way into the coolest stories. She'd met Rachel during her adventures, and they'd been roommates and bandmates ever since. Plenty of men had tried to pin her down through the years, but she never let them.

It wasn't just her own fate at stake here. She knew Betty was happier without Dan than she could ever be with him.

"Is that why you're with me?" Dan said. "To get back at your sister?"

"No, I..." Betty said.

Joey could see the wheels turning in her sister's mind. She wanted to speak up and say what it looked like to her, but knew Betty had to get there on her own.

"Maybe I did," Betty said at last. "I was so angry, and I've loved you for so long, and I thought I loved you that way. I think I do. I don't know. I thought how great it would be to see Joey's face when she came home and saw us together, but I didn't expect you to propose."

Betty began to cry, and Joey instinctively wrapped her arms around her. She knew what it felt like to be eighteen and in love and jealous and a million other emotions at the same time.

"It's okay," Joey said, as Betty cried harder on her shoulder.

"Is it?" Dan said.

"Oh Dan." Joey looked up at him from over Betty's head.

"You left me to go be with someone else," Dan said. "She was only with me to get back at you. I need to get out of here."

"Dan, wait," Joey said, but he grabbed the keys next to Betty's purse and walked out.

"Go after him," Betty said, wiping her nose with her sleeve.

"Are you okay?" Joey said.

"I'm fine. Really. I screwed this all up, but I'm fine."

Joey hugged her sister again as a thunderclap sounded and scared them both.

"Sounds like a storm is starting," Betty said. "Go catch him before he drives away in it. I'll clean up and we can go somewhere nearby until it passes. We all need to talk."

"Okay, thanks," Joey said, running for the door.

She cut through a shortcut she knew would lead her to the parking lot, hoping it would save her enough time to catch Dan before he left. It was pouring rain and she could barely see, but she thought she could just make out his profile about thirty yards away.

"Dan! Wait!" she yelled as she ran in his direction.

She didn't see if he turned around and she definitely didn't see the small pile of river rocks that had been kicked out onto the sidewalk. Rocks plus sudden rain can lead to a slippery situation.

And that was her last thought before everything went dark.

CHAPTER FORTY-ONE

WHEN SHE OPENED her eyes, she was wet and had a headache. That made sense. What didn't make sense were all the voices surrounding her. And none of them sounded like Dan.

"Joey? Can you hear us, sweetie?"

Joey tried to focus on the three faces above her, but she couldn't place them. Then not being able to place them made her realize who they were.

The reunion. She was back at the reunion and looking up at her three former classmates whose names she couldn't remember. In what must have looked like an insane thing for her to do, she reached her hand up and felt her right breast. It was clearly the chest of a thirty-eight-year-old mother of three.

"*Joey?*" a new voice entered the small space, but it was one she definitely knew.

"Betty!" she said, trying to sit up, but realizing how lightheaded she felt.

"Hey! Are you okay? They said you fell or something." Betty knelt beside her.

"She tripped on my screen," said Mary Fate. "I'm sorry. I thought I had enough room in here."

Joey looked around to see the screen that had been dividing the tent had fallen over. She must have caused quite a ruckus when she took it down.

"But what was behind it?" she said.

"Oh, I made this game," Mary said excitedly. "You pick something from the first category, and it tells you your fortune."

Joey watched as Mary grabbed the laptop that had been sitting behind the screen and typed VALENTINE into the open text bar. She hit enter and the screen popped up with the following:

> *You marry Devon Sawa*
> *You have two cats*
> *You live in a mansion*
> *You vacation in Switzerland*

"See?" Mary said proudly. "It's like that old MASH game, but I program it differently depending on the age group. Just a fun little reunion game. Big hit with the Boomer women who get to marry Elvis."

"Ooh, fun!" said Betty. "I wanna play!"

"Uh, can someone help me up?" Joey asked.

"Oh, right," Betty said. "Upsie-daisy."

The other three women had already exited the tent, and Joey and Betty followed them onto the gymnasium floor, but Joey steered them to an empty table.

"Ouch, that looks like it hurts," Betty said, staring at Joey's forehead.

"I'm fine," Joey said.

She was definitely fine, physically anyway. But mentally, she knew she'd need some time to get her bearings. Everything seemed to be exactly as it had been before she'd gone into the tent. How much time could have passed? Could what had felt like a year for her really have only taken thirty seconds?

"Betty, are you happy?" she said suddenly.

"Uh, yeah?" Betty said. "Why do you ask?"

"Did you ever wish you could have married Dan?"

"Ew. That would be like marrying my brother. Literally."

"But I mean, before. When we were kids."

"I mean, sure. You know I had a crush on him, but it was always supposed to be you two. And no offense because you know I love you guys, but you're both way too boring for me."

Joey laughed and really looked at her sister. They wanted

different things in life and that was okay. More than okay. They were both living their best lives. Joey only wished Betty could find someone to settle down with.

Rachel. What if she was supposed to be with Rachel? Joey looked up at the stage where the band was doing one of the songs Betty didn't sing lead for and wondered for the first time if they were more than just roommates.

"Are you and Rachel together?" Joey asked, opting to be blunt.

"No, I mean, kinda." Betty looked annoyed. "We are sometimes, but sometimes we're just roommates."

Joey had no idea how this arrangement might work, but she realized she didn't care. Betty was happy and had someone in her life in the way she wanted someone. She'd been so focused on her own life lately she hadn't even noticed her own sister settling down. Sort of.

Speaking of her own marriage, she was desperate to see Dan. Even aloof, infuriating Dan was better than the heartbroken version she'd just left behind.

"I have to go home," she said, standing so fast her head spun.

"Let me drive you," Betty said. "You look a little wobbly."

"No, I'm okay. I just need to find my purse."

"Here you go," came a voice from behind her. Mary Fate was holding her glittery Kate Spade clutch and offering it to her.

"I know you'd hate to lose this," she said, winking.

"That lady is weird," said Betty as Mary walked away.

"You have no idea," said Joey.

CHAPTER FORTY-TWO

JOEY THREW THE front door open a bit too hard, causing it to slam against the wall in their entryway, but she didn't care. She now knew how Dorothy must have felt after coming home from Oz and even with a clumsy entrance and aching head, there was no place like home.

"Dan!" she called as she kicked her shoes off and ran up the stairs. It was still early, but he'd been so tired lately. She opened the door to their room and called his name again, more gently this time.

And there he was. Her Dan. Not Betty's. Not anyone else's. He was staring at his phone, but looked up as she came in, eyebrows raised with questions.

She caught a glimpse of herself in the mirror and knew at least a few of those would have to do with her disheveled appearance. It made her laugh. Now he was going to think she both looked and sounded unhinged.

"Are you okay?" was the first question Dan decided to go with.

"Are we okay?" she said, closing the distance between them quickly and leaning down to give him a hug.

She knew she'd sound deranged if she explained everything that had happened. Or, rather, she knew she likely was crazy, so either way, best to try to stay in the moment.

"Look, I know you agreed we should talk, and I think I know why," she began.

"Do you have a bump on your head?" he said, still taking in the full picture.

"Yes, but I'm fine. Just took a little tumble at the reunion."

"Is that why you're back so soon?" He reached up to touch the bump gently.

"Yes, kinda. I also think I know what you've been wanting to talk about with me, and I wanted to say that I'm not ready to give up."

He looked immediately taken aback and she knew she'd hit on the issue at hand.

"I know things have been off between us for a while," she said. "And I'm not saying it will be easy, but I think we can work through this. One tough year is no reason to throw everything away."

"Wait, what?" he said, now sitting up across from her on the bed.

"I don't want to get divorced." Joey finally let the tears she'd been holding back fall.

"Who said anything about getting divorced?" Dan looked genuinely confused.

"You...said we needed to talk?" Joey knew he had said it, but his reaction wasn't making sense.

"We do. But not about divorce. I can't believe you...you thought..."

Joey was shocked to see his shoulders heave as he looked down at his hands. He'd been so distant for months now and even though she hated to see him cry, she was relieved he was showing emotions again.

"Hey, hey," she said. "I'm sorry. I just thought... I mean, you've barely looked at me and just seem so angry all the time. When you said you wanted to talk, I thought you were going to leave me."

"I'm so sorry," he said, looking back up at Joey.

There. Joey wasn't sure what had changed, but there was the Dan she'd spent most of her life married to. Had she imagined it all? No, that was silly. He had been pulling away for months. She couldn't remember the last time he had laughed with her. But what could have changed in the last few hours to bring that to an end?

"I haven't been feeling like myself for months," he said. "At first, I thought I was just tired, but then every little thing seemed to bother me. And I took it all out on you."

She nodded, crying a bit, but trying to keep it together so he'd go on.

"I thought it was all in my head, so I started seeing a therapist once a week," he went on. "I know, I didn't tell you, but I was mad at you some days and just needed someone to talk to about it. And I know I was only mad at you because you were responding to how I was treating you.

"We talked through a lot of things, like how I'm dealing with getting older, and that I was feeling so tired all the time. She told me I should see my doctor to get a full physical. I brushed it off, but then I fell asleep at work one day and realized I should probably listen to her."

Joey tried not to bristle about hearing all of this for the first time after months and months of being shut out, but he was sharing now, so she grabbed his hand and said, "Go on."

"My doctor ran a bunch of tests and agreed that something seemed off. We started with a new diet because I mentioned that my stomach's been hurting, but it didn't seem to help."

"I wish you'd talked to me," Joey said. "I've been going crazy. And I could have helped you with all that."

"I know. I stopped being mad at you and knew we should talk about everything, but then my doctor started sending me to see specialists and I didn't want you to worry until we had some answers. There were so many diagnoses to eliminate and the last thing I thought you needed right now was to be doing a bunch of Google searches for scary diseases that I don't even have."

Joey laughed and snorted at the same time, semi-choking on her own tears. It broke the tension for them both and she leaned into him for another hug, thankful he had worked through things enough to come back to her.

"So, are there any scary diseases I *should* be looking up?" She took the tissue Dan was handing her.

"No," Dan said.

"Thank God," she said, before blowing her nose.

"You shouldn't look anything up because we know what it is."

The tone of his voice made her body go rigid.

"Tell me."

"Joey, I love you for real."

"Oh my God, just please tell me," she pleaded.

"It's colon cancer, stage four."

And for the second time that night, Joey felt everything go black.

CHAPTER FORTY-THREE

THE CANCER WAS too advanced, he'd told her. He'd been to multiple specialists and there was nothing they could do. His last hope had been an appointment today with a doctor who had a reputation for being a miracle worker.

"So, what's our miracle?" Joey asked between sobs.

"Our life together," he said. "Joey, you and the kids have been my miracle."

Joey was crying too hard for more questions and knew she wouldn't get better answers tonight anyway. Dan was a fighter. If he was telling her this news like this, she knew it was over. Suddenly, her decision to come back, if she'd actually made it, felt like the only thing that made sense. Losing Dan was unthinkable. She couldn't let herself think what it meant for her life right now.

She was here to walk beside him through this, and to be strong for their kids. And she would do exactly that.

"We should go away," she said.

"We should what? Are you okay?" he said.

"I am the least okay I've ever been in my life. But if our time is running out, I'm not going to spend a single second of it crying."

He gave her an incredulous look and they both laughed.

"Okay, I am obviously going to cry. A lot," she said. "But I know what my life is without you, and I don't want to spend any time thinking about that while you're still here. And while you are still here, I want to go away. Just you, me, and the kids. Let's spend our summer in London. People can visit us to say goodbye, but only if you want them to."

"I think you're in shock," Dan said. "Let's talk about this tomorrow, okay?"

She nodded and laid down next to him on the bed, then sighed as he wrapped himself around her. Was she in shock? Honestly, after the whole time-traveling experience and now Earth-shattering news, she quite likely was. But she was also thinking clearly and knew that if Dan was turning down treatment, it was because he wanted his last few months to be as happy as possible. They had planned to visit London on his fortieth birthday. Why not go now?

Somewhere in the back corners of her mind, her brain was trying to get her to grieve. To panic. Her husband had just told her he was dying. She should be a wreck right about now.

But in the same way she knew Dan would be stoic until the end, she knew she would be the one who brought the joy to their family. Those were the roles they had always played, and she could think of no better course of action than to keep the status quo. Whenever she wanted to panic, Dan had always been the one to balance her anxiety with a blanket of calm. And when things got tough, she found a way to walk her kids through it with humor and the simple thought that they could get through anything together.

There would be days ahead where she could fall apart. There would be years for that, in fact. She was going to be a widow before she turned forty. Other than losing her kids, losing Dan had always been her worst nightmare. But now she was facing it, she felt an almost eerie sense of calm. Losing Dan to cancer felt somehow easier to bear than him leaving her by choice.

That was clearly the denial talking, but she wore it like a shield.

She smiled as she felt Dan's breathing become rhythmic and knew he was asleep. He'd always been able to do that, and she was always so envious, but not tonight. Tonight, she had plans to make.

She gently tried to sneak away, but somewhere in his sleepy state, Dan held her more tightly as she inched her way to the edge of the bed. And since her nights of sleeping in his arms were numbered, she gave up and instead decided to try to memorize everything about this feeling.

Dan's arms were strong. She reached her hand up to touch the one he had wrapped around her and realized it wasn't as big as she remembered. Come to think of it, Dan's whole body didn't feel like it had before. She had thought he was losing a little weight, but as they hadn't touched in months, she hadn't pieced it all together until just now.

As much as she had blamed him for their issues of late, could she really pin it all on him when she had somehow missed that he had cancer? How oblivious do you have to be to miss those signs?

Had it been the same way with Taylor? Taylor told her over and over again they were so young and she wasn't ready for a big commitment. And what had Joey done? Proposed. Yikes. She'd been given a second chance to go back and do things better and apparently hadn't learned a thing.

And poor Dan. In one timeline, he got dumped by both Joey and Betty, and in another, he ended up dying of cancer. Well, he would have died in that other one, too, she guessed. If it had been real. It certainly felt real. *What even is reality anymore?*

Either way, Joey remembered what she had said to him at the apartment in the alternate timeline. If she could have another chance, she'd spend the rest of her life making it up to him. Even though it would now just be the rest of his life, she wanted to do everything she could to live up to that promise, even if he'd never heard her make it.

Somewhere between deciding she was a terrible, oblivious partner, and trying to think through the space-time continuum, Joey finally fell asleep.

CHAPTER FORTY-FOUR

JOEY WOKE WITH the dawn the next morning with a new sense of purpose. She was excited. And of all the emotions one might expect to feel the day after learning their spouse was dying, she realized that had to be at the bottom of the list. For happily married people, anyway.

She started making phone calls as soon as offices started to open, and by the time Dan came down, she'd taken over the kitchen table with her computer, printer, and the dozens of things she'd already printed.

"Okay," she said, waiting for Dan to take the whole picture in before she bombarded him with details. "Here's where we are. We can afford to go to London indefinitely. You've always wanted to go. I don't think we should wait."

She showed him everything she'd printed. They'd been such good savers over the years that Dan's retirement account had more than enough to cover the trip, and his life insurance would help her get by when he was gone.

"But this is all assuming your doctors are correct," Joey said. "I'm not ready to believe that and I think we should at least stop by a couple clinics in Europe..."

"Joey," Dan said. "I don't want to spend my last few months with you in a hospital."

"Right, I know. Just one clinic? We don't have to check you in. Just a couple tests to see if they agree with your doctors here. They're supposed to be one of the best places in the world for treating colon cancer."

"One clinic."

"What time are the kids coming home?" Joey looked around at the mess she'd made.

Dan glanced at the clock on the wall behind her. "About thirty minutes," he said.

Joey's heart leaped at the thought of seeing her babies again. Well, they weren't babies. Elizabeth was eighteen and getting ready to head to college, another thing Joey was in denial about. Shawn was sixteen and had been taller than her for about three years now. Meghan was fourteen and like all little sisters before her, eager to prove herself outside of her siblings' shadows.

"We have to tell them," Joey said. "Today."

Dan nodded and they both began clearing the kitchen table to make space for what would be the worst family meeting of their lives. The grief monster, as she was now calling that voice in the back of her brain, crept his way into Joey's conscience, but she used all her mental strength to tell him to shut the hell up.

"I think we should tell them about London too," Dan said as they waited for their brood to return from a weekend away.

They'd all attended the same music camp that Joey, Taylor, and Betty had, and were getting ready to be counselors there this year. Elizabeth drove them all to training and orientation weekend, and Joey realized she'd have to call the camp to tell them they'd be down three staffers this year.

Joey wanted to run and hug the kids as they came in but knew that teenagers were like cats. If she went to them, they'd pull away. Always better to let them come to her.

"How was it?" she said as they came in through the garage, stopping by the laundry room to drop their dirty clothes.

Elizabeth, the empath, came into the kitchen first and immediately picked up on the general vibe.

"What's wrong?" she said.

Meghan came in behind her, ears perked and eyes wide. "Huh? What, Lizzie?"

Shawn walked in last, clearly just waking up from the car ride home.

"Chill," he said to his sisters. "Mom and Dad are just standing by the table awkwardly because that's where they like to stand."

"Kids, could you come sit with us for a minute?" Dan said.

"Oh my God," Elizabeth said, putting her hands to her mouth and starting to cry.

"What, Lizzie?" Meghan said, her own tears starting to form in solidarity.

"You're getting divorced!" Elizabeth said through sobs. "I knew it. I knew this was coming."

"No one is getting divorced," Joey said, shooting Dan an *I-told-you-so* face.

The kids relaxed enough to join them at the table and Dan began with an apology.

"I know I haven't been myself lately," he said gently. "And Lizzie Boo, I'm so sorry if how I've behaved made you think we were getting divorced. I wish you would have talked to me."

Joey smiled at her eldest girl, so much like her father. She'd seen enough in the past few months to know something was wrong, but tried to deal with it herself, just like Dan had.

"I owe you all an apology," Dan said. "I wasn't feeling well and took that all out on the people I love the most. It's not an excuse, it's just what happened. Do you forgive me?"

The kids nodded, but Elizabeth still clearly had her guard up.

"Then what's this all about?" she said.

"There's no easy way to say this," Dan said. "But I wasn't

feeling well because I have cancer. It's advanced and…"

His words were drowned out by Meghan's primal wail, then Elizabeth's sobs. Shawn sat there, stunned, but pulled one sister to each of his shoulders and patted their heads while they cried.

The grief monster swallowed Joey whole and she let herself break down. If everyone else was going to cry right now, she might as well too. When they had all caught their breath, Dan explained what the doctors had said.

"Treatment might buy me a few extra months, but they would be miserable months," he said.

The kids looked horrified but nodded. They'd all seen what cancer could do to a person as different family members on both sides had gone through chemo or radiation. It was worth it for people who had a chance to recover, but Joey knew she'd be making the same choice if it had been her instead of Dan.

"So, what do we do?" Shawn asked.

"Well, we obviously want to spend as much time together as we can," Joey said. "And since Daddy's always wanted to go to the UK, we thought we'd spend the rest of this summer in London."

The kids looked back and forth at each other, then at their parents.

"London," Meghan repeated. "When do we leave?"

They all got up from the table and surrounded Dan with a group hug, then scattered with instructions from Joey on how best to help prepare for the trip. There was laundry to do, passports to find, calls to make, and barely enough time to do get it all done before they left.

And as Joey looked at Dan, she knew there would never be enough time.

Chapter Forty-Five

THE FIVE SHAWS landed in London on a beautiful sunny day. Joey loved London in the rain, but she was excited to introduce her family to the city in perfect weather. Dan was extremely impressed with how well she was able to navigate them to the house she'd rented, and she wondered how long they'd believe she'd picked it all up from research.

She wondered how long she'd be able to convince herself, really. The time she'd spent in London with Taylor might just have been a dream, but that didn't explain how she knew her way around a foreign city she'd never been to before. She tried not to think about it because she still felt a little crazy, but still, it was...odd.

Joey left the first couple of days open for them to just acclimate to the new time zone and make sure Dan felt well enough to explore. Other than being a bit fatigued, he seemed like the same old Dan, and Joey was eternally grateful that they still had time where everything felt normal. Other than the kids each bursting into tears at different parts of the day, they seemed like any other American family on holiday.

On their fourth day in London, the kids went out on their own while Joey and Dan arrived at his appointment with the National Colorectal Health Center. They were shown to a room where Dan could rest between tests, and Joey pulled the travel Scrabble she'd brought along to pass the time and began to set it up on the small table near the bed.

As different people showed up during the day to take Dan to his next round, Joey curled up on the bed and pressed Dan's shirt to her face. She wondered how many of his shirts she could get him to wear, but not wash while they were there. She didn't want to lose the smell of him. She didn't want to lose him, period, but that didn't seem to be something she could control.

"All done, mate," a cheery attendant said, escorting Dan back to the room. "The doctor will be in shortly to speak with you."

"How are you feeling?" Joey asked, reluctantly handing him his shirt so he could change.

"Tired, but fine," he said. "Mind if I join you?"

"I'm not sure there's room." She moved her body all the way to one side.

"I could always just climb on top of you." He raised his eyebrows.

They both giggled as he did just that and Joey felt like a teenager again. There was something about first kisses and almost last kisses. She wished she'd cherished each one in between but knew that was almost impossible.

Dan felt her tears on his face and propped himself up so he could look at her.

"Don't get your hopes up, okay?" he said. "Any time they can give me here is just a bonus. We go on with the plan either way."

Joey was ready to protest when the door opened and she buried her face into Dan's chest, mortified to be caught in bed with a boy for the first time in decades.

"Don't stop on my account," the doctor said, cracking up with laughter as Dan jumped out of bed and Joey awkwardly followed. She turned her back to him as he introduced himself to Dan, frantically buttoning her blouse and trying to pull herself together. As they made small talk behind her, Joey realized she'd heard that voice before.

She turned around to see if the face matched the voice and gasped.

"Liam!" she exclaimed.

"Do I know you?" he said.

Oh no. Of course he didn't know her. How could she explain that she knew his name? And how was he even real?

"Sorry," she said. "You look like someone I used to know. Hi, I'm Joey."

"I look like someone you know who is also named Liam?" he said, still searching her face for any sign of recognition.

"Is that your name too?" she said. "How strange."

The men continued their introductions while Joey pretended to look something up on her phone. As Dan filled Liam in on his history and what the other doctors had told him, Joey tried to slow her breathing.

Even though Dan had asked her not to, she felt all the hope she'd been burying way deep down come back into her heart. She had once helped Liam by convincing Will to marry him. Maybe all of that had happened so he could be the miracle to save her husband? It was a stretch, to be sure, but why else had fate brought them together again?

She looked at Liam's left hand as he read through the reports from Dan's tests. He was wearing a wedding ring. She wondered if he was still with Will. She hoped he was. But not as much as she hoped he had good news for them.

"I've reviewed everything we did here today," he said. "And I'm sorry to say we don't have any treatments that will save your life."

Joey willed herself to stay strong. She pictured herself giving the grief monster the finger.

"But," he said, "we do have some experimental treatments that will help you with energy and pain in the time you do have left. You'll want to stop by here for bloodwork once every few weeks so we can see how you're progressing, but my other patients who are using it have felt great, right up until the end."

Joey brightened at the thought of this. Dan had already made his peace with the inevitability of his situation. Maybe Liam's miracle would be comfort, and not a cure.

"Thank you, Doctor," Dan said, standing to shake his hand. "My family and I will be here as long as we're able. If you can help make that time easier for us all, I'm incredibly grateful."

Joey knew it was weird, but she hugged Liam anyway. They'd shared a lot together whether he knew it or not. And even though it wasn't what she'd hoped for, he'd given them a light in the darkness too.

More energy meant Dan could venture out farther away from the flat they were renting than they had planned. Pain management meant those adventures could actually be enjoyed. She understood what Liam meant by "progressing." With the pain and fatigue masked, Dan would be okay until all of a sudden he wasn't.

But Joey didn't want to think about that right now. She had an adventure to plan.

Chapter Forty-Six

"WHAT'S IN CORNWALL?" Dan asked as she finished telling them all about what she had in mind.

"I don't know," she lied. "It's just pretty."

She tried to blame her obsession with wanting to take them all there on the movie *About Time*. It was Dan's favorite movie, after all. But since his diagnosis, none of them had been strong enough to watch it.

"Trust me," she said. "I think the sea air would do us all some good."

As much as they all loved London, this point was hard to argue. None of them had ever lived in a big city before and the prospect of open spaces near the water was appealing.

And after only two days on his new medications, Dan's energy had really perked up. If they were going to get there, it should be now. She found a house near where Will's family lived because it was the area she knew best and rented it for the weekend. It overlooked the sea and looked absolutely gorgeous in the pictures.

As soon as they arrived, the rest of her family finally acquiesced and told her she'd been right. The house had Adirondack chairs out back and they all couldn't wait to sit and soak up a bit of sun. Her poor desert children were looking practically pasty outside of their native habitat.

She'd arranged for five bikes to be waiting for them at the house and after double (read: triple) checking that Dan was feeling up to it, they rode into town for lunch.

"I could totally live here," said Shawn as they set their bikes against the wall of the café.

"Maybe you will," Joey said, reaching up to put an arm around her son. "You could buy a nice cottage and turn it into a B&B."

"What about college?" he said.

"Honey, you only get one life," she said. "Make it everything you want it to be. Make it extraordinary."

She wasn't sure how much wisdom she could impart on a sixteen-year-old boy, but she did know that Dan's cancer had changed her kids already. They were smart and mature for their age, but the way they looked out for one another since they'd heard the news had Joey convinced they were going to be okay once he passed.

Not that it would be easy, but they would get through it together. And that was enough.

As they finished their lunch, Joey nearly had a heart attack as she looked across the room. There, sitting at a table with a woman and two small children, was Will.

Oh no, she thought. Without her, Will and Liam must never have gotten married. At least the kids and woman looked nice, but Joey was so sad to think that Will had never come out and lived like he wanted to.

Or maybe that whole timeline was wrong for everyone, and by not talking Will into saying yes to Liam, she'd saved them a horrible divorce or something. She thought about this for a while and didn't realize she'd been openly staring at Will until he waved at her.

Did he recognize her? Was that even possible? Without a word of explanation to her family, she got up and went to his table.

"Do you know me?" she said.

"I don't think so," Will said.

"Oh, but you waved."

"I wasn't sure if you were staring at me or having a seizure," he said with a laugh.

"Oh, goodness. I'm so sorry. You just remind me of someone I used to know."

"From here?"

"Uh, no, London."

"Ah, well, sorry, miss. Enjoy your holiday."

"Thank you," she said. "You have a beautiful family. I'm sorry to bother you, Will."

She turned around quickly, hoping she'd said his name so quietly that he didn't notice.

"Did she just call you Will?" the woman with Will said.

"Miss?" Will said. "How do you know my name?"

"Oh, I, uh, heard your wife say it earlier," she said. "When I was accidentally staring at you."

This seemed to appease him, but he gave her the same look Liam had as she tried to will all the blood to drain from her face.

"Sister," he said.

"Excuse me?"

"This is my sister," he repeated.

"Oh," Joey said.

And since they already thought she was crazy, she decided to press her luck. "But these are your kids?"

"Yes, these are my kids."

"And you're married?"

"I am."

"To?" she asked.

"My husband's name is Liam," he said, with a face that looked like annoyance and amusement.

"I'm so happy to hear that," she said, before walking away for real.

"Do you know them?" Dan asked when she sat back down.

"I thought I did," she said.

"You watch too many British movies," Meghan said. "Everyone here looks familiar to you."

They all laughed, and Joey felt joy mix with foolishness. How big of a narcissist did she have to be to assume that everyone's lives would just fall apart without her? Will and Liam hadn't needed her to sort things out. She wished she could go back and ask for their whole love story, but it wasn't hers to know. They were together and that was all that mattered.

And if they were real, and really together, that meant the rest was maybe, possibly real too.

CHAPTER FORTY-SEVEN

JOEY, DAN, AND the kids returned to London from Cornwall with an exciting week ahead of them. Elizabeth had asked to be put in charge of their next activities and Joey couldn't wait to see what she came up with.

Dan stopped by the clinic first for a blood draw and was cleared to keep on living. He'd lost a little bit of weight, but that was normal.

The first group of family members from back home were scheduled to arrive the next week and the kids were excited to show their grandparents and Aunt Betty around their new city. In the meantime, though, it was just the five of them and Joey was loving every minute of it. They played games, did puzzles, walked to restaurants, walked to parks, and just *lived.*

Their first night back, Elizabeth announced that she'd gotten them all tickets to see a new play in the West End. It was a musical about a wood sprite who falls in love with a human boy, or something like that. It was supposed to be really good and even if it wasn't, just seeing a show in London was an experience that Joey wanted to share with her family.

They arrived at the show about twenty minutes before curtain and Joey pulled the ultimate mom move and told everyone to go to the bathroom before it started.

"So we won't have to go in the middle of the show," her kids said in unison. They could roll their eyes all they wanted. She'd never forgive them for making her miss half of *The Lion King* when it came to town. She'd had to take all three of them on three separate potty trips. Never again.

As she waited in the lobby for the girls to join her, Joey flipped through the program absentmindedly. Something caught her eye on one of the pages, but Meghan came out just then and she forgot to look again. As they took their seats for the show, Joey squeezed Elizabeth's hand.

"Thank you, sweetie," she whispered.

"Thank you, Mom," she replied.

The show started and Joey did what she always did at the theater. She looked at her kids' faces and watched their reactions. Dan's too. She was aware of what was happening on stage, but especially now, she was much more interested in her own family than anyone on that stage.

Or so she thought.

Midway through the first act, she heard the low, sweet sound of a cello solo. She assumed it was coming from the pit, but saw Dan cock his head as he looked at the stage. She followed his gaze and saw that a woman was on stage, playing the most beautiful song on her cello, which was decorated to match the stage.

The woman's face was nearly covered by her long hair, cascading over her and her instrument, but Joey could just make out her nose and lips. And she knew them in an instant.

There was just enough light from the stage that she could barely read her program. She flipped to the center for the cast list and confirmed what she already knew.

Taylor, she mouthed at Dan, who noticed her frantically checking her program.

No way, he mouthed back.

They both turned to look again, and Joey felt silly for not realizing who it was from the opening bars. The cello was a beautiful instrument, but it sounded different depending on who was playing it. She didn't used to think so, but Taylor could play her dozens of recordings and Joey always knew which ones were her.

Once again, she felt like Dorothy returning from Oz. She still wasn't sure if she'd actually gone over the proverbial rainbow, but she could hear herself pointing from Will, to Liam, and now to

Taylor.

And you were there! And you were there! And you were there!

Taylor might not remember everything they'd shared in alternate 2002, but Joey hoped she'd still remember her from when they were kids. She'd never had a chance to say goodbye before her dream ended and she felt oddly unsettled. And as happy as she was to see Will and Liam doing well, she had to know how Taylor's life had gone in her absence.

As the show ended, Joey asked an usher where the cast might greet people after the show. He directed her to the outside area where fans could ask for an autograph.

"Do you know, by chance, if Taylor Page greets friends after the show?" she said, worried that she might not get enough time to talk if she was in a crowd.

"What's your name, love?" he said. "I'll go and ask."

Joey waited but told Dan and the kids they could head home if they wanted to. Before they could leave, the usher was back and said Taylor would like to invite Joey and her family backstage.

Elizabeth was thrilled that her plans had turned into such a special event, Meghan was walking like she owned the place, and Shawn tried to pretend he wasn't gawking at the scantily clad dancers who had joined Taylor on stage during the show. Dan offered to just say hello, then wait for her in the lobby. She could tell he was tired and promised to keep it brief.

"Nonsense," he said. "I'm just a little sleepy. Past my

bedtime."

They knocked on Taylor's dressing room door and Joey opened the door when she heard the words "come in."

"Joey!" Taylor exclaimed, stopping in the middle of removing her stage makeup to stand, leaving half of her face still covered.

"Taylor!" Joey said, walking forward to hug her. She was oddly thankful that Taylor looked a little messy. It helped her heart rate slow. A bit.

She introduced Dan and the kids, then said she'd be out in a minute.

"What are you all doing in London?" Taylor said after they'd gone, sitting back down to finish the makeup removal process.

Joey filled her in on Dan's cancer, talking as fast as she could. It was hard enough to keep the grief monster at bay if she thought about it. Talking about it was a whole other story.

"But tell me, how are you?" Joey said.

"Oh, Joey," she said. "I'm so sorry. I won't say another word, but here's my number in London. You guys call if you need anything while you're here. Theater tickets, dinner reservations, anything."

Joey took the piece of paper and pocketed it, thankful to move away from the subject.

"I'm married," Taylor said. "Another cellist, if you can believe it."

"That's wonderful," Joey said. "I heard you met someone

when you were in France, right?"

"Actually, I met her here. She was visiting my freshman year and we didn't hit it off right away, but then we worked together in Paris and we've been together ever since."

Vienne. Joey didn't have to ask, and she didn't want to make a fool of herself again in London by accidentally revealing too much information.

"I'm so happy for you, Taylor," she said. "And thank you for your number. It's nice to have old friends nearby."

"You know something?" Taylor said. "I had a crush on you back in the day. And not just at camp."

"I know." Joey blushed.

"Ugh, was I that obvious?"

"No, but I do want to thank you for the valentine you sent me. I'm sorry I never mentioned it before, and that I left you waiting that day."

Someone else knocked on the door, distracting Taylor and reminding Joey that her family was waiting. They hugged goodbye before one of Taylor's castmates came in, and as Joey was about to leave, Taylor said, "I don't think I ever gave you a valentine, by the way. Guess you must have had two secret admirers."

Joey laughed and walked out but felt herself shaking. She opened the note in her pocket and studied Taylor's handwriting. She'd been writing quickly, but it looked nothing like the girly letters she remembered. Her brain was swirling with thoughts, but they all vanished as she took in the scene waiting for her in the lobby.

On a chair by the exit sat an unconscious Dan, surrounded by three terrified children.

CHAPTER FORTY-EIGHT

"RELAX, GUYS, I was just dehydrated," Dan said the next morning for what had to have been the twentieth time already. It was only nine a.m., but they'd all been fussing over him all night.

The theater staff had already called for help by the time Joey got to them in the lobby and after a quick stop by the hospital for an IV, they were sent home with orders for rest and more water. Joey knew he was fine, or as fine as he could be under the circumstances, but she and the kids were still pretty shaken up.

Even though his bloodwork had been okay just yesterday, Joey didn't want to take any chances. She called home and told their family to get there as soon as possible, just in case.

Careful planner that she was, Elizabeth had made her second

day of activities a light day, assuming correctly that her dad might need some downtime. All they had to do was get to Abbey Road and take a picture in the crosswalk. She had the route mapped out, but Joey gently suggested they hire a car to get them as close as they could, then take them straight home.

Because Elizabeth was raised on the classics, she was a huge Beatles fan, and had also arranged for them all to dress as one of the Beatles. Since they were five, not four, they'd have two Ringos, she explained.

It was a brief, but fun excursion and Joey knew she'd cherish the pictures forever. When they arrived back at the house, Dan went straight to the couch to lie down. The kids took turns sitting on the cushion under his feet, and Joey knew they could sense that he'd taken a turn.

She excused herself and went to her bedroom to call Liam.

"I don't understand," she said when she reached him. "His levels looked fine yesterday."

"They did," he agreed. "But even one bout of dehydration can be a big deal right now. Keep him hydrated and let him sleep today. If he doesn't bounce back tomorrow, we'll come by and see about making him comfortable."

Joey knew what that meant and felt herself panicking. They were supposed to have more time. Months, maybe. Had this trip been a terrible idea? If they were still at home, would everything be okay? What if she'd taken Dan straight to Mary Fate? Could she have sent Dan back in time to catch the cancer early and stop this all from happening?

No, that couldn't work. Nothing she had done in that timeline had changed anything in her current one.

The grief monster sunk her claws in and tried to pull her down, but Joey resisted.

Not yet, she told herself. Dan was in the next room and so were her kids.

By the next day, Dan had bounced back, just as Liam had predicted. They weren't out of the woods, but they could all breathe easier as Dan joined them at the table for breakfast.

"Kids, how long will I love you?"

"As long as stars are above you," they replied together.

"And longer if I can," Joey said, finishing the line from one of their favorite songs. It was a pattern they'd picked up when the kids were little, and the brief moment of normalcy lifted them all up.

Joey looked over at the couch where Dan had spent all day yesterday and last night and was fully relieved they'd come to London. If that had been her couch and he had died on it, she knew she'd burn it. A morbid, but important question popped into her head.

"Dan, where do you want to die?" she said.

"Holding your hand," he said. "All of yours."

"Doesn't matter where?" she said.

"Not as long as I've got you." He looked right at Joey but

blinked back tears. "And kids, I held your hands the day you were born. I'd be honored if you'd return the favor by holding mine as I go."

They all cried but promised him that they would.

And that's just what they did. Days later, holding Joey's hand with his left, and all three kids' hands with his right, Dan took his last breath as his favorite version of "Over the Rainbow" played. Leave it to Dan to create his own death mix CD, and to somehow manage to go out on the song he had hoped to.

Their extended family made it in time to say goodbye but gave Joey and the kids a front row view when the time came. And as much as she knew her heart would never heal from losing Dan, she was immensely thankful that she'd been there for every occasion in his life, including its end.

She no longer fought to keep the grief monster at bay, but instead welcomed her like a friend. The kids had their own grief monsters and Joey could almost see the moment they shifted. From now on, they would categorize their memories in two columns: with Dad, and after Dad. She could already feel it happening to herself.

She didn't know what the After Dan column would hold, but she had promised to live for them both, hours before he died.

And so she would.

CHAPTER FORTY-NINE

THE FUNERAL WAS on a Monday. Joey had chosen the day because she typically hated Mondays and didn't see any reason to forever ruin one of the other six days. Dan had requested a celebration of life, with very specific music requests throughout. No one was to wear black and everyone was to take shots. Well, not the little kids, anyway.

As Joey got dressed in a pink, sparkly skirt Dan had always loved, she looked around for the matching bag. It wasn't on her shelf, and she remembered why not with a laugh. She'd dropped it on the floor in her room after the reunion and...

"Aha," she said, pulling it out from under the bed. She brushed away a few dust bunnies from the glitter exterior and looked inside.

Ahh, there's my lipstick, she thought. She rooted around to see what other items she had shoved in there that night. Gum, Dan's copy of the car keys (oops), some cash, and two mystery items she had to pull out to see.

She nearly fainted as she pulled them into view. She was holding the ring she'd bought for Taylor from that antique store. The ring that had only existed for her in a timeline she had convinced herself did not exist.

The other thing she'd pulled out was a thumb drive that looked like the one she'd used during her time in London. But it couldn't be. Could it?

If the ring was real, then was she holding the books she'd written? She'd thought they were gone forever, or at least until she could sit down to try to rewrite them. She plugged the drive into her laptop and opened the folder. They were all there, including her nearly finished, more personal novel, that she now knew exactly how to end.

She sat and took stock of her life. She was on her way to bury her husband. It was the ultimate con for her list, to be sure. But she had promised that same husband to live for them both. What would Dan have done with more time? What would she have wanted him to do?

Looking down at her laptop, she knew at least one thing she was going to do. But it would have to wait.

She slipped the Art Deco ring onto her right hand, again knowing she'd need something to help keep her centered. She took one last look in the mirror, silently commanding her reflection to keep it together, then went to rally the kids and head out.

After a few songs played over a slideshow, Pastor Matt, a friend of Dan's, offered everyone gathered a chance to pray and remember Dan's life. To Joey's surprise, he then called Betty up, saying she had a letter to read.

"Dan asked me to read this," she said, already losing the battle to hold back her tears. "I have no idea why, because I'm going to cry, but here we go:

> *Friends, family, people who feel obligated to be here, and those of you who just came for the food,*
>
> *I have lived an extraordinary life. Since you're here, you might agree with that. Or maybe you just think it was an okay life. But hey, it's my party, and I say it was extraordinary. My life began thirty-eight years ago, but I didn't start living until I met the beautiful woman who would become my wife, my Joey. And I didn't understand the meaning of life until she gave me our three incredible kids.*
>
> *Elizabeth, my Lizzie Boo, you are so much like your old man. I'm proud but want you to be a little more like your mom, if you can. I know it's hard to share your feelings,*

but when you find the right person, I want you to tell them how you feel every single day.

Shawn, you are my son shine. I know I don't have to say this, but I want you to look after your mother and sisters now. But I want you to let them look after you too. Being a man doesn't mean pretending you don't have feelings and being brave doesn't mean you're never afraid.

Meghan, my Megaroo, you are so strong, mentally and physically. I pity anyone who underestimates you. Don't forget to let that guard down, though, from time to time. You can't get hurt if you don't let anyone in, but it's no way to live. Open that big heart of yours, baby girl.

Joey, what can I say? I had a dream the other day that we didn't end up together and let me tell you, baby. It sucked. I know you're being so strong for the kids right now, but don't be afraid to fall apart together. They're going to look to you for cues on how to handle this and I don't mean to put pressure on you, but hope you'll remember to show them that you're not okay either. I'm amazing. Of course it'll be hard to get over me. Pause for laughter.

"Oops, I wasn't supposed to read that part," Betty said.

When you're ready, I want you to write. You are the most gifted writer I've ever known and I'm sorry if I ever made you feel like anything less than that. If your grouch of a husband could have gotten his head out of his you-know-what from time to time, I would have told you that more. I should have supported your dreams more. Just know I'm cheering you on, from wherever I am, Joey. I love you for real.

Speaking of which, I hope you find someone to spend the rest of your life with. I hate to leave you so soon, and thought I'd hate the idea of you with someone else. But as my time runs out, I realize asking you to live for us both doesn't mean you carry me around like an anchor. Carry all that love you've got for me into your next great love.

As for the rest of you, thank you for everything we shared. Especially that one thing. You know what I'm talking about. Yeah, that was fun.

I'll miss you all. Do me a favor and think of me when you hear this song.

All my love,

Dan

Joey held her breath, wondering what Dan had chosen for his final goodbye song. And as "Thong Song" began to play, she laughed so hard she almost peed her pants. Or maybe she actually did. Just a little.

The service rolled into a wake with lots of food and music. Joey did her best to circulate in the room and found herself thoroughly exhausted by the time the last few guests were leaving.

"Joey?"

She turned to see a familiar-looking woman standing near her but couldn't come up with her name. It had happened a few times that day, but none of her kids were close enough to rescue her as they had before.

"I'm not sure if you remember me," she said. "We went to high school together. I heard about Dan and just wanted to pay my respects."

"Thank you so much," Joey said. Her voice was so familiar, but still, no name popped into her head.

"I also know this is a weird time to mention this. But not sure when I'll see you again, so I just wanted to see if you remembered getting a valentine back at CHS? From a secret admirer?"

"It was you?" Joey gasped.

"Yeah. I know it's silly, but Dan's letter said we should tell people how we feel. And I think you're amazing."

"Lori!" Joey said, matching her face to a name at last.

"Oh!" Lori said, laughing. "Oh my gosh, I didn't say my name.

Yes, I'm Lori."

Joey had too many thoughts hit her brain at once. She probably had a really strange look on her face as she tried to process them, so Lori said, "Sorry, I'm not trying to hit on you at your husband's funeral. I should go."

"No, you can hit on me anytime," Joey said. "I mean, no, that's not what I mean. I think what I meant to say is we should get together sometime, so can I get your number? But I'm going to need some time."

"Of course." Lori took Joey's phone from her and added her number.

They hugged goodbye and Joey knew she wouldn't call Lori right away, but maybe after a while. She needed to grieve, needed to take Elizabeth to college, and wanted the whole family to start counseling sessions as soon as they could. But for the first time since Dan had said the words "stage four," she could see something beyond the abyss that Dan's loss represented in her brain. What she had thought was never-ending despair now looked more like a chasm she could maybe build a bridge over, someday.

But in the meantime, she had a book to finish.

Acknowledgements

This book would not exist if not for the love and support I've received from friends, family, colleagues, and the strangers at the grocery store who gave me a pep talk that one time (true story).

Brittany Velasquez and Nicole King—my biggest fans and constant cheerleaders; I love that my writing process has always been to type "the end," and then send your way.

Mom and Dad—I'm so thankful that you have always supported my dreams and I know you're proudly looking down at your baby girl, Daddy.

Casie Bazay and Amanda Woody—I'm so thankful we connected on Twitter. To have the support of other writers has been a lifeline in this process.

Elizabeth Coldwell—your guidance with edits and the whole publishing experience is more than I could have hoped for.

To the entire NineStar team—thank you for taking a chance on me and loving my stories as much as I do. Here's to the next adventures together!

ABOUT SHANA SCHWARZ

Shana Schwarz is a careerwoman by day, writer by night, mother at all times to three incredible children, wife to a loving husband, and the author of *As Long as Stars Are Above You*. Born in San Diego, California, she now hails from Gilbert, Arizona where she especially enjoys giving back to her community by volunteering at schools, libraries, with Girl Scouts, and any causes that benefit marginalized communities, especially LGBTQIA+ youth. She began her career as a writer at the age of 17 when she was hired to cover movies, arts, and features for a youth-oriented page in the *Arizona Republic*. With twenty years of writing experience for magazines, newspapers, social media, and more, she is thrilled to have her first novel out in the world.

Facebook

www.facebook.com/ShanaSchwarzAuthor

Twitter

@shanaschwarz

Website

www.nerdygirlapproved.com